TAFADZWA GWETAI

Yvonne Vera

Without a Name and *Under the Tongue*

Yvonne Vera is one of Zimbabwe's best
known writers. She was born in Bulawayo,
where she now works as the director of the
National Gallery, and is the author of *Butter-
fly Burning* (FSG, 2000). In 1997 she was
awarded the Commonwealth Writers Prize
(Africa Region) for *Under the Tongue*.

WITHOUT A NAME

and

UNDER THE TONGUE

WITHOUT A NAME

and

UNDER THE TONGUE

Yvonne Vera

FARRAR, STRAUS AND GIROUX
NEW YORK

Farrar, Straus and Giroux
18 West 18th Street, New York 10011

Without a Name copyright © 1994 by Yvonne Vera
Under the Tongue copyright © 1996 by Yvonne Vera
All rights reserved
Printed in the United States of America
Without a Name originally published in 1994 by Baobab Books, Zimbabwe
Under the Tongue originally published in 1996 by Baobab Books, Zimbabwe
Published in the United States by Farrar, Straus and Giroux
First American edition, 2002

Library of Congress Cataloging-in-Publication Data
Vera, Yvonne.
    Without a name ; and, Under the tongue / by Yvonne Vera.— 1st American ed.
    p. cm.
    ISBN 0-374-52816-0 (alk. paper)
    1. Zimbabwe—Fiction.   2. Young women—Fiction.   3. Incest victims—
Fiction.   4. Pregnant women—Fiction.   I. Title: Without a name ; and, Under the
tongue.   II. Vera, Yvonne. Under the tongue.   III. Title: Under the tongue.   IV. Title.

PR9390.9.V47 W5 2002
823'.914—dc21
                                                                        2001023286

Designed by Lisa Stokes

www.fsgbooks.com

WITHOUT A NAME

FOR MY MOTHER
AND HER MOTHER

Heat mauled the upturned faces.

The bus was fierce red. Skin turned a violent mauve. That is how hot the day was. The faces jostled and hurried, surrounding the bus with shimmering voices. The large black wheels were yellow with gathered dust. Mud had dried in the wide grooves within the tires. Small stones looked out from the mud. Thick layers of brown earth covered the windows and the rest of the body, but the bus still shone red. It was that red. It was so stunningly red it was living.

Mazvita separated herself from the waiting red of the bus, color so sharp it cut into her thought like lightning. Merciless, that red. It was an everywhere red which cracked the white and black shell of her eyes. Heat thundered beneath her feet. She retreated.

She stood apart, anxious, waiting for the doors of the bus to burst open. She watched the door closed tightly against her entry. The bus sat in a rippling lake of rising heat and dust. The dust sucked the water from her eyes.

"Nothing to load onto the bus?" the voice swooped toward her. It did not wait for an answer but swept past and landed on the trembling roof of the bus; it belonged to an agile black shape fastening beds, caged chickens, maize sacks, chairs, and tables. The pile on the bus was growing steadily. The bus shook, and sagged. The bus sat still. A loud shout rang through the air, concerning a mattress about to fall. The shape that was the conductor left one end of the bus and slid to the back, pulled hard at something gray hanging and heavy, retrieved it, and tied it straight down the roof.

Mazvita saw the faces hurry, heard a murmuring like boiling water. The voices swirled like a flood to one end of the bus where there was space left to haul one more article. A bed was raised high toward the roof, brought forward, tied down. It was lost among the many pieces already struggling there. Jarring, voices scrambled and jostled. Cries converged, called, and retreated.

Mazvita felt the intense heat which circled her with the simmering voices and brought the red glow of the bus to her face. The ominous hue spread down her arms, and sought her fingers. She stood still. She stood near the bus shelter, but not beneath it, a metal roof held up by four high wooden poles. She stood still. She stood next to one of the poles, on the outside. She stood on the outside. She stood alone.

Beneath the dim shed, children had been left to guard the smaller possessions which would be carried onto the bus but their attention wandered as soon as the bus enveloped their mothers in its vibrant shade. They exploded. They ran around the shelter, screeched and scattered. They laughed, because one of them had fallen down. The shed was full of their delight. They rescued each other from beneath fallen bags which, filled to capacity, tore open on their collapse. A red scarf lay trampled on the ground. It wove itself around a bare tiny foot, and the figure fell again in a knotted cry, but the children had discovered the secret of their freedom; there was no need for caution or restraint. There were no pauses to their joy which resounded in one continuous voice, a tender elegant quiver pure and plain. The children found gaps between the rays of the sun and ran through them, their tiny bodies supple, carried on pattering flirtatious feet, in faltering voices that embraced their yearning for enchanting discoveries. They found narrow and untrodden paths. The children had a limitless tenacity for dream, a flowing capacity to wander wide and far. They were children.

They emerged from their escape in a myriad of joy, their faces covered with their gaiety, bright with their phenomenal journeying. They held out their cupped hands above their heads and gathered the joy that tumbled from the sun, which swooped down their throats. Blue lizard tails disappeared beneath the gray roof of the shed, vanished between their fingers which were spread out to the sky. They ran back quickly into the shed, gurgling, their fingers still surprised, burning and tingling. They filled their dreams with unformed desires, with tentative aspirations, with timid bliss. They bathed in an exhilarating caress of innocent and weariless joy. Then they fell on the split bags, and slept an accented sleep.

The shrieks reached Mazvita, climbed over her shoulders to her back, receded. She felt a violent throbbing cross her forehead, and lifted a limp hand to wipe the water from her face. Drops fell from behind her ears, slid slowly down, trickled beyond her shoulders to her back. The water traced a convoluted path over her tired skin. She passed the back of her right hand across her neck and spread the warm sweat over her arm, over the loose skin. Her neck was twisted. A bone at the bottom of her neck told her that her neck had been turned and turned till it could no longer find a resting place. Her neck had been broken. She felt a violent piercing like shattered glass on her tongue, where she carried fragments of her being.

There was a lump growing on the side of her neck. A sagging grew with the lump, so that her body leaned to the left, following the heavy lump. She could no longer swallow even her saliva, which settled in one huge lump in her throat. Whatever she swallowed moved to one side of her body. She had lost her center, the center in which her thoughts had found anchor. She was amazed at how quickly the past vanished.

The lump had swallowed her thoughts, she decided. She blamed this lump for her inability to think clear thoughts. It swelled endlessly, this lump, and she leaned her head further toward her lowered shoulder, as though she needed a new angle to her reality, an untried advantage, her eyes quiet, tucked upward beneath her eyelids. She peered at her reality. Some unusual sight had appeared before her, gripped her face and smeared it with mud. The mud had dried in angry and repeated streaks across her whole face, over her lips, her forehead, and held her in a puzzled and frenzied stare.

She nursed an elbow gently in her palm, and waited anxiously. The lump lay between her ear and her shoulder. She felt it growing there in repeated outward pushes. She had no doubt that all her body was moving slowly into that lump, that she would eventually turn to find her whole being had abandoned her, rushed into that space beside her neck, for she heard voices there. She heard a faint dying cry. The fingers on her left hand curved slowly upward.

Her skin peeled off, parting from her body. She had suffered so much that her skin threatened to fall pitilessly to the ground. It hung from below her neck, from her arms, from her whole silent body. The skin pulled away from her in the intense dry heat. She felt it pull from her shoulders. She screamed, her arms and elbows bare. The sky tore with her scream, for a dark cloud appeared suddenly over her eyes, blinding her. The skin fell from her back. She was left stripped, exposed, bare wide across her back.

She leaned backward, her eyes astonished.

~

They had spoken, among the mushrooms.

The mushrooms stood meek beneath the decaying log that was partly buried in the ground, and she had bent forward and touched them fearfully, touched their floating beauty, for they seemed ready to break, seemed waiting to break if they were touched. They were white beneath the cold black shadow, the wet earth, the decay. They were a radiant white like drops of daylight. Their rim touched the ground with a curving soft shell. A dark soil grew threateningly over the feathery shelter of the mushroom.

Mazvita had moved from the brightness to the shadow and the shadow was so sudden and heavy like water thrown over her arms, over her whole waiting body that she shivered at the water that fell from the tree not in drops, but in a sudden spilling, like the mushrooms which she sighted when she turned her face laughing and gay, seeking to find him. The water pulled at her arms in thick and heavy waves. It felt heavy over her arms. She moved eagerly toward the log.

A lush greenness spread to the ground. It was wet there, and the ground was soft. The large tree glistened with wide thickly veined leaves. The leaves were rounded partings of green moon. The trunk stood firm and straight, with a smooth gray surface. The bark was wound in stiff tightening circles spiraling to the base, disappearing in a mound of weaving roots that swirled angrily from the ground. Within the roots, which formed small channels and basins, was held some water with a swarm of brown decaying leaves. Branches grew outward, flattened, spread, and created a broad dark circle, a wide shelter. Her shoulders tingled with the suddenness of the cold. She looked up at the merging leaves where there was no sky; the shadow cleansed her. There was no sky under the tree.

The laughing made her curious and careless, made her want to pull at the mushrooms, so she reached her thumb and forefinger ever so delicately, and held the soft cushiony head, held it so gently, feeling already the grooved underneath so tender and the surface above so smooth that her finger slid over the head past the grooves and met a thin polished stem, soft, then she held that stem tight but gentle, pulled at it tight but gentle. The ground was soft and yielding.

There was nothing like pulling that mushroom. It accepted her gentle hand, followed her in a long slow quiver and the stem grew out of the ground into her palm. White. The neck was smooth and waiting and soft. She felt the softness linger between her fingers, slippery, fragile. The soil crept beneath her nails.

It was after she held it in her palm that she saw the brown spots within the grooves, the spots that spread to the smooth surface of the mushroom, a sad brown quite unexpected. The tinge spread downward, toward the neck. She felt the loss of that whiteness and longed for the bright sun, away from the cold shade. Above her she heard the leaves move softly over each other. She held the neck of the mushroom between her fingers. She looked up and searched beneath the cold leaves for a waiting sky.

Nyenyedzi caught up with her. She saw him come and held out the mushroom to him, and he took it and crushed it, crushed its soft head.

"It could be poisonous," Nyenyedzi said. He crushed the mushroom against her palm, with his right hand. "I will find mushrooms for you, if you want some. This mushroom is not for eating."

"I wasn't going to eat it." She shrugged her shoulders. "I only wanted to touch it. It felt so good to hold it. Why did you crush it?"

"There are many under the log." He kicked at the log. It surrendered decay, turned hollow. Crumbled pieces fell toward the soft heads of the mushrooms below, tarnishing them. She wanted to gather the mushrooms toward her. She held out her palm, but did not move. She remembered the mushroom he had crushed. She held out a trembling palm. She was hopeful.

He named her. He reminded her of what they had found together, for he had held her, and she had grown toward him, yielded from the ground into his palm.

It was not difficult.

The blaze she felt amazed her when all there was afterward was a lingering wet and delicate softness beneath her. She smelled the decaying leaves surrounding the rotting log, and kept the crushed mushroom in her hand as he found her waiting, found her. The stem was still whole, a neck closed and rounded. She was grateful he had not broken the neck and held it tight within her fingers. Her palm grew warm.

He touched her below her neck, above her firm breasts, and she curled her arm over his back, rested her hand there. She rested a closed hand over his back where a thin trickling sweat met her fingers. With her other hand she gathered the warmth beneath his arm and spread it in slow deliberate motions across his back. She listened. She heard the leaves turn silent. She listened. She heard him murmur "*Howa*." She was sure he had called.

"Is that what you called me?" Mazvita asked, thrilled, surprised, still longing.

"I don't remember. Is that what I called you?"

"You said *Howa*, twice. I'm sure I heard you. Is that what you called me?"

"I called you . . . *Howa*." He laughed.

In the future Nyenyedzi evoked that name when he wanted to hold her close, like today. She always thought of the spotless white mushrooms she had not found.

He held her. He brought to her soft dying mushrooms, the ones she had found.

~

three

The white aprons hung on a corner of the street. Two wooden pegs had selected one wide square apron and pinned it along a small wire held between two poles, one of them a parking meter which said in a red flash "expired." There was a bright red car parked there. The other pole was a small boy's arm. He stood as though in possession of a secret. He was quite still for such a strenuous and monotonous task. He stood as though frightened to move. The woman seller cast unkind glances at him. He held one end of the white apron, so that it opened very wide, and the wind blew on one side of it, and it curved inward as though in anticipation of the baby.

The back of the apron was heavily stitched, turning it into a firmly padded support. The back was starched, cracked like bark. Somewhere the white thread had run out and the tailor had employed a black thread. This black thread ran frantically through the borders of the white apron, zigzagging. It was meant to be endearing, but the suddenness of the contrasting thread held the eyes in a furrowed gaze. It was truly surprising.

The boy had tied the bottom of this ingenious apron to his right leg. The boy simply stood, as though it was in his nature to stand. His feet were planted firmly on the ground. His hair stood in proud and independent strands all over his head. One arm hung limply above the pocket of his torn shorts. One could have walked forward and put a coin through his ear. He was the same height as the meter, equally still. The meter was silver gray, so was the boy. Perhaps he had not eaten for days, months, maybe years—he competed with the meter for thinness. The apron shone a dramatic white against the boy's thinness, against his face dull and gray.

People pushed and shoved as though they had no eyes to see. It was 1977, what else was there to do but push forward. Mazvita walked quickly through the impassive faces, in a tunnel of her own where it was truly unlit, desperately narrow. She sent her head forward through the tunnel and met a darkness tall and consuming, where she could not turn or speak or see. She could no longer move her head forward because the pain threatened to collapse her whole body, to sink her into the ground, to bury her. She held her head in a definite yet unaccountable stare.

In an instant, she had turned blind, the blindness rose from inside her and overwhelmed her entire face. She no longer spoke. Mute and wounded she moved through the streets and wept. Her weeping fell in silent drops into her cupped palms. The streets grew rich with showers, with her tears.

Mazvita turned from one end of the street into another, and the aprons greeted her. "Apron, *Amai!* Apron, *Amai!*" A commodious and enterprising woman shouted at her as she turned, as though she expected her. It was the first voice Mazvita recognized since morning. The voice was anxious and pressing.

Mazvita bought the apron in a state of quiet nervousness. Her fingers trembled, not yet certain whether to confess or escape. Some kinds of truths long for the indifferent face of a stranger, such truths love that face from the neck up, from the forehead down. There is little to remember in a face with which no intimacy has been shared, to which there is no kinship. There is nothing to lose between strangers, absolutely no risk of being contaminated by another's emotion; there are no histories shared, no promises made, no hopes conjured and affirmed. Only faces offered, in improbable disguises, promising freedom.

The apron was made of strong cotton material. In this matter, Mazvita was not going to take any chances. She had regretfully unfolded four lonely silver coins from a dirty handkerchief held in a crumpled lump between her fingers. She had purchased the apron in the middle of a busy indifferent street.

Her fingers, as they handed the coins over, loved the stranger's face. They caressed that strangeness anonymously, confided in that absent sensibility. Mazvita's fingers folded and unfolded while waiting for the apron to be unhooked from the fence. The seller imagined that this particular apron was what this particular stranger wanted, because she had moved determinedly toward that apron. But Mazvita had only moved forward because she felt like falling down, felt like spreading her arms wide. Mazvita searched the woman's face as she prepared the apron. Mazvita stood still.

The boy kept his arm up. Morsels of freedom desperately snatched were bitter, soaked with a remorseful aftertaste. It was not worth the effort, the risk.

Mazvita moved on, the apron folded close to her breast. She looked for an unlit passage.

~

four

An egg, the brown of its tone, the unforgettable pale invitation of its color, the maze of its smells, the promise of fragility like anxious tenderness. The rainbow of its smooth endearing surface, elegant, its echoes slender and oval. Its promises hidden but complete, its palm-nestling size, a shy silent awakening. Supple and wholesome.

He held her hand and walked between the rocks where the earth was dry, leaving the egg where they had found it. The bird had built a nest in a crevice within the rock.

"Mazvita," he said freely.

The rocks towered above them, near and rounded. Underneath were dull shelters. Dense shadows cast by the looming stones, like smoke. The rocks were smooth. Brittle and jagged stones peeled off the rocks and fell to the ground. Mazvita and Nyenyedzi walked out to a rock that was spread on the ground. Short green leaves grew between meandering cracks. Within the hard stone were the tight swollen roots of trees, and desperate waving stems of slowly growing plants.

Mazvita pulled Nyenyedzi down beneath the rocks which had been warmed by the sun, and felt the warmth rise over her naked back. She held him in a succumbing gasp, then folded his head over her chest. She felt the hardened skin of his knee over her pelvis, felt it scratch briefly beneath her navel. The knee pressed down on her, but not painfully. So she passed a tender finger through his hair. He lay between her fingers. She closed her eyes against the blue that fell from the sky into her eyes and she heard a sentinel on a rock cry loud, a piercing cry that beat against her ears.

The sentinel cried yet again, slow and chasing, one call calling another. The sky overwhelmed her with a lithe blue hanging over her eyebrows, so near her breath embraced it. The blue pulled her up into the sky, and she called softly to tell him about a translucent shiver that tumbled from the sky, about the daze that lulled her in a horizon prolific with caressing yellow rays, about the warmth rippling over her knees, but he smoothed her stomach in tender fond waves and she forgot about the blue of the sky about his knee about . . . She was breathless with an ancient longing. He smoothed her back with a kind tongue, blue and large like the sky. She felt a brilliant cascading joy. A calm modest thrill sent an even pressure to her palm then circled her bent wrists, resting in the wet spaces between her fingers. She felt the ground, exquisite, pressed at the back of her feet. The blue brimmed and soared around her. She was restored in a pleated sky.

He moved above her in lilting repeated spasms. He held her very close, wiped her forehead in gentle beseeching strokes. He rested a solid arm on the ground above the soft curve of her shoulder, beside her ear. She felt the inside of his arm rub firmly against her, along her neck. He was content with her presence. Their eyes met in a silence rich with imaginings, with a brave ecstasy. He was heavy where he rested above her, but even in that she found an exultation so complete and final, an ease unquestionable, a profuse tenderness. There was no beginning or ending to her happiness, only a continuous whirl of blue cloud. The air was bright and clear beneath the sky, transparent. A dazzling shower of bright stars fell from the sky. She was comforted. They lay still in a triumphant arch, under the spread hem of the horizon, intertwined. They lay in a whispering veil of white and lucid cloud.

She remembered the egg, whole, nestling on her palm.

∾

five

Harare.

Mazvita found a welcoming alley between two towering brick buildings. The alley was narrow and cramped. *Nyore Nyore*—one side of the walls promised falsely. A thick smoke descended into the constricting crevice, and swallowed some of the letters. The bricks had turned from bright red to a rapid black brown. *Nyore Nyore.* Letters shouted, struggled beneath growing layers of plastering smoke. It was that kind of era. An easy wealth was promised, an easy love, an easy life, an easy death. *Nyore Nyore.* The alley smelled of tentative promises quickly betrayed. It smelled of urine.

A frayed leather purse lay abandoned on the edge of the building. A black hat, the brim torn off, curled stiffly upward. Pigeons fluttered gray spotted wings and flew from the entrapping cavern, frightened by her feet. They returned, retreating behind the set of lined metal garbage cans. Wings settled into a slow cloying palpitation.

Mazvita met empty cans of beans, where broken bottles littered the narrow path, amid the garbage cans. One can folded in the middle. It had been thrust into the alley in one heaving and merciless maneuver. The wall had met it with equal indifference. The world vacillated with clamor. Recognition was easy, calm, tumultuous. Poverty was not a secret; otherwise what was there to clamber out of? It was necessary to be poor. It made people long for a long day full of greetings.

The pigeons beat a sorrowful liturgy with rippling wings and quivering feet. They sent brittle cries that soaked into the mounds of metal rubble. Mazvita walked gingerly through the mounting debris, casting one brief glance over her shoulder. She heard a cat leap in the dark onto the roof of the *Nyore Nyore* building. Wood lay discarded in the alley, some broken furniture, a broken chair with one leg missing and the seat fatally collapsed. The chair had been mangled. One half of its backrest had folded forward, unable to sustain the havoc on its frame.

Mazvita stood amid the wreckage, halfway through the dimness. She searched the brittle ground. She witnessed people walk past each end of the alley. The people lasted only two quick steps before they disappeared on either side. Her reality was that brief and intermittent. She gasped at her vision full of chaos. The people dwindled into mere shades of color and cloud. She thought she saw an umbrella walk by. Just like that. Then she saw a soldier. It frightened her to see the soldier. He must have a gun. After all it was 1977. Guns were pointed to the sky.

She hated the city and its commitment to a wild and stultifying indifference. She pulled her eyes from the streets, from the stilted portions of her world. She rejected the silhouettes and the figures. Her eyes withdrew; she heard them fall deep in her head. Water rippled secretly into her ears.

Mazvita unfolded the baby from the towel. She unwound the towel from her back, peeled it off the back of the child. Mazvita let the towel drop softly, behind her, to the ground. The towel was dirty. It was soggy with the heat. Mazvita circled the baby with her arms, and held it down. She bent slowly forward and the baby moved slightly along her waist, toward her left. She bent further forward and prepared to receive the baby from beneath her arm, under her left shoulder. Mazvita felt the baby in her armpit. She gasped. She waited.

Wings beat past, and rested. Mazvita was startled. The bird rose, disappeared beneath the wreckage. Mazvita lingered with closed eyes, her heart pounding, her elbows pinned to her sides, over the quiet legs of the baby. She searched the end of the alley and again saw the people pass by, in rapid dots, in specks of memory. Knees trembled and bent toward the ground. Mazvita held her muscles tightly, firmly, urgently. The baby grew heavy on her back. Mazvita bowed, yielded to the searing pain. She waited. Mazvita heard a faint murmur move from herself to the baby. She told the baby to keep still. She turned to her right, slid the baby gently but quickly into her waiting hands, in the front. Her hands waited eagerly for her baby. She felt the baby fall in a lump into her hands. Mazvita tightened her eyes. The moment was rich, it filled her arms. The baby fell from her back and rested across her stomach, its legs spread rigidly around her waist. Mazvita raised her back and opened her eyes wide. She saw the baby.

She looked at the top of the child's head. She dipped a sole finger into her mouth then passed it gently over the child. She rested her finger shakingly on the child and remembered. The past came to her in rapid waves that made her heave the child forward, away from her, in a deep and uncontrollable motion of rejection. Her arms shook and she held the child still, like flame. She returned the baby slowly to her stomach and touched again the child's head with a wet finger. She pressed gently the top of the child's head, murmured softly, cooingly. She whispered to the child to close its eyes, whispered in an elegant dying lullaby, then she crumbled suddenly to the unwelcoming ground. Mazvita fell hard on the ground. Knees collapsed but she held tightly to the baby, pulling it close to her breast. She fell backward into the mounds of filth and decay and stale water. The moment filled her arms and she held tightly. Pigeons clamored out of their enclaves. Mazvita clutched the baby, cried steadily, silently, curled her legs inward.

She took the baby and placed it gently into her waiting leg, amid the drifting papers and echoes of ululating wings. Armpits sweltered, pulsating sadly. Mazvita was truly alone.

She held the baby over her leg. She raised her bent knee high, away from the ground. The bottom of her leg, her ankle, supported the rest of the child. The child's body curved inward, as though its back was broken. Mazvita opened the apron wide. She carefully spread the apron over the crook of her right leg. She performed the task deliberately, lingering over each motion, smoothing the cloth into a shiny evenness. It was warm and sweaty within her leg. She felt the sweat grow stickily over her skin. She was grateful. She still breathed, could move forward toward her destination. What did it matter what she suffered?

Where her bent leg met the left, she transferred the baby quietly to the wide spread cloth. She transferred the head of the baby to the white silent apron. The baby lay encased within the embroidered stitching. The baby was sewn up there. She could not do much about the wild stitching though her heart rose against it. She rested the head on the apron, and waited. The child pressed hard on her knee. Mazvita raised her knee gently from the ground and brought the child close to her face. With faintly pleading lips Mazvita felt the forehead of the child.

She gathered her strength in repeated quiet sighs that escaped from her dry lips. Something had sucked the water from the roof of her mouth. It was dry like a pod. She moved her tongue around her mouth, in circles. It felt like a flattened and dried fruit.

She breathed hard, absorbing the stale air in the alley, the sound of rustling paper, of car hooters piercing the darkness. She breathed the poverty and the loneliness, the black walls tarnished and buried with the cries of abandoned dreams, of apparitions of laughter fueled with desperation, of voices pained. She breathed vigorously the darkness of the alley. She breathed, in an exhilarated effort to secure her own survival, to rise to her feet, to carry the moment solidly in her arms.

Mazvita turned and looked over her shoulder. She turned yet again and looked. She looked. The sound grew thick, made rich the darkness. She swung forward, her head suspended above the child, swung forward. She bent over the child and touched it with her forehead. She swayed far to one side, returned smoothly to the other, above the child. She bent forward, over the head of the child. There was release. She held herself up from the ground. Mazvita braced for the journey.

The silence was temporary. She had to move fast before the harrowing intrusion came back, haunting and persistent, haunting and truly her own. In one pleading effort she raised her neck. Her face jutted angrily forward. She expected not mysterious visitations, no changes to her world. She only pulled her neck high in an effort to detach her head from her body, somehow, to walk around with her body completely severed. Her thoughts would be free. It was the constant nearness of her head to the child that made her frenzied and perplexed. There was not enough space between her and the child she bore on her back. If she could remove her head, and store it a distance from the stillness on her back, then she could begin. She would be two people. She would be many. One of her would be free. One of her would protect the other. She wanted one other of her, that is how she conceived of her escape. She attempted this enigmatic separation by drawing mightily forward, by dropping her chest down, by pulling her arms to the back, by restraining her shoulders. Her neck rose upward and she felt a violent pain delve downward to her back. She looked up.

She looked up and saw a white sky clear and untarnished, beyond the rooftops. The suddenness of the sky surprised her. The whiteness folded into the alley, squeezed down over the rooftops, near and white. She welcomed the sky. The brightness broke into her eyes. It was a fervent cloud and it lingered. Mazvita did not hurry. She kept the moment for as long as she could. She felt light. She felt lifted from the darkness, light, out of the darkness. The cloud fell downward, very near to her, then it passed, uncovering a gray and torpid roof. Her eyes were vivid with tears. Her head sank down, down. The sky grew pale. She turned back to the baby and lifted it up, together with the apron. She lifted the baby up above her head, and freed her legs. She freed her legs upward, forward, straight. She uncurled her back and stood upright, she bent forward, she slid the baby's head and the apron over her left shoulder onto her waiting back. Her back shivered, not with cold. A tremendous unbearable ripple. She felt the baby settle familiarly over her back. Yesterday frightened her with its familiarity.

She felt the baby's head beneath her neck, and she moved her body briefly, to center the baby along her frame. The baby settled on her back. She pulled the stiff legs of the baby, resting them along her twisted waist, and tucked the apron beneath the baby, then she pulled the bottom ends of the apron tight against her stomach, pulled the top down, and the two sets of strings met in the middle of her breasts. She tied the bands together. She made a tight knot that threatened to sever her across the middle. She tore hard into her breasts with the apron bands.

The apron pulled hard at her neck, strangled her last breath. She continued to tighten the knot, though the bands were already shortened, and no further movement could be secured. She pulled at the stillness, hard. The stillness made her pause in her pulling, and she listened to it. The stillness made her entire body tremble but she nurtured that stillness because it was hers. She held long and patiently. The cloth tore at her skin, into her palm. She did not protest the pain. She preferred that continuous strangling. It kept her awake, the suffocation, it kept her alive and desperate. She tightened the firm bands, and recovered herself from the debris, from the shelter and secrecy.

She searched the ground in furtive glances, with a twisted and narrowed brow, with shaking limbs. She moved forward though the air held her in a ferocious grip. Her back tightened, and she moved forward, away from the narrow passage. Mazvita moved forward.

Milk poured from her breasts. It fell in soured lumps.

~

"Nyenyedzi," she whispered and he looked toward her.

She recognized his back though he wore the bright green overalls, like all the other men in the tobacco barn. It was a busy place. The bales of tobacco arrived early in the morning in long trucks and the workers carried them into the shed. They held their arms forward. They heaved. They moved forward. The bales sat in sections marked throughout the hall, in high piles taller than the men. There was a strong smell of decay throughout. It was dark and damp inside where the leaves were tied together with rope, tied tightly together. The thick rope cut through the thickened leaves and the leaves bulged in angry circles. The leaves swelled outward, away from the rope.

At the end of the day Mazvita felt weak, felt faint and frantic from the tobacco smell which spread toward her, like decay. The tobacco rose from inside her. The air was moldy. Dark and wet. She turned her eyes toward the asbestos roof where the air hung downward like soot. It choked her, that smell. Out of the shed, she breathed slowly and preciously.

The storehouse was not far from the farm itself. She had worked on the farm, but now she made tea in a little kitchen behind the storehouse for the foreman and his assistants. She missed the bright open fields where she had worked, but now that she was closer to Nyenyedzi, she did not mind the dark. It was dark in the shed.

The bales lit the place with a decaying glow, with the strong biting scent. She looked forward to the end of the day when they left the shed and walked through the forest to the edge of the farm, to the huts. Nyenyedzi walked with her. She feared the forest, and the war. Nyenyedzi did not mind taking her into the forest, after work. He had no fear of the war.

"Why did you leave your home?" he asked. "You are not from Kadoma."

"I needed work. I heard there is always work on the tobacco farms. I am from Mubaira, in Mhondoro."

"We must go back together to Mubaira."

"I can never go back there."

"Why?"

"The war is bad in Mhondoro. It is hard to close your eyes there and sleep. It is hard to be living. I left because I want to reach the city. I cannot return so quickly."

"We must go back. I want to meet your parents."

"It is kind of you, Nyenyedzi, but it is hard to find words for certain things. I really must go to the city. One day I woke up in a mist, you know, the kind you enter with your shoulders. The morning seemed to rise from the ground, because the mist was so thick and spread slowly from the ground. Even the sun turns white at dawn, in that mist. My arms were heavy as I walked in that early morning to carry water from the river. I only had my arms, because my legs were buried in the mist, but I felt the mist moving upward, toward my face. It was strange to walk separated like that. Then I felt something pulling me down into the grass. This something pulled hard at my legs, till I fell down. I saw nothing, because the mist was so heavy. I tumbled through that mist, screaming into the grass. I had forgotten about my legs. It was a man that pulled me into that grass. He held a gun. I felt the gun, though I did not see it. After that experience, I decided to leave."

They walked on, silently, along the path.

"We should live together and cook together," Nyenyedzi said suddenly. "This is a good place for us to live."

"I cannot live here. We must go to the city and live there. I don't know if we are safe even in this place. The war is everywhere. We must go to the city. It is said there is no war there. Freedom has already arrived. Do you see the people who come from the city . . . they have no fear in their eyes. Look at how frightened we are here. Can freedom arrive here the way it has arrived in the city?"

"In a big place like that. We will be lost. We will even lose one another."

"No. It is the perfect place to begin. It is better there than here. Harare. The news about the freedom in that city has reached all the ears in Mubaira. I am waiting to make enough money, then I will go on the bus. It will be easier in Harare. You can forget anything in the city."

"You can forget your own mother. I cannot go to Harare. I like the land. I cannot leave the land and go to a strange unwelcoming place. I have heard terrible stories about Harare. Everyone carries a knife there. A knife that you can fold and place in your pocket. A knife that you can open quickly when you are in trouble. Imagine a place with such a knife. Then there are those robbers called *skuz'apo*. They empty your pockets before you can blink. They take a knife from your own pocket and kill you with it. You cannot even trust your shadow in a place like that. Some people have robbed and killed their own parents in that place. What kind of a place is that?"

"I have to see this with my own eyes. I am going there, Nyenyedzi."

"No. I cannot go there. I have worked here for two years now, and I know this place better than you do. I was born not far from here. You have not lived here long and say you are leaving. If you stayed a year we could make decisions. We could go to Mubaira first and meet your parents. The city will bury us."

"I must move on. I will move on."

Mazvita carried a strong desire to free herself from the burden of fear, from the skies licked with blue and burning with flame. She had not told Nyenyedzi everything. She had not told him about what that man who pulled her down had whispered to her, how she ran through the mist with torn clothes, with his whispering carried in her ears, how the sky behind her exploded as the village beyond the river burned, and she shouted loud because her arms reached forward, but not forward enough to rescue the people, to put out the flame, and she cried and ran with her two legs missing, buried, and she thought she ran with her arms because she saw them swing forward, swing back, swing forward, carry her through that mist toward the huts which mingled with the river and her crying, then she fell down, looked beneath the mist at the burning hut because the mist had lifted, now formed a canopy over her head, and she discovered her legs, whole, beneath her body, and she discovered a large circle of bright yellow sun. Waiting, burning, naturally.

~

seven

Harare.

Newspaper headings covered the dark alley, promised no freedom to the agitated people. But there were ample signs of the freedom the people had already claimed for themselves—empty shells
of *Ambi*, green and red. The world promised a lighter skin, greater
freedom. It was 1977, freedom was skin deep but joyous and tantalizing. *Ambi*. Freedom was coy and brash, spread between palms,
shared and physical. Freedom was a translucent nose, ready to
drop. Freedom left one with black-skinned ears. A mask. A carnival. Reality had found a double, turbulent and final. Freedom
spoke from behind a mask, but no one asked any deep questions,
no one understood what freedom truly was. To be sure, it was
boisterous. *Ambi* would do for now, certainly. No one questioned

the gaps in reality. If there was a gap anywhere, there was an opening too. Freedom was any kind of opening through which one could squeeze. People fought to achieve gaps in their reality. The people danced in an enviable kind of self-mutilation.

Freedom squeezed out of a tube was better than nothing, freedom was, after all, purchasable. It was sensual, and that was to be longed for, procured even if the cost was nothing less than one's soul. Such negotiations were easy. It was risky to carry a soul in the city streets, as Mazvita had discovered. In Harare, it was best to sell your soul to the first and easiest bidder. In this one case of the *Ambi Generation* at least one received a permanent mark for the exchange, an elaborate transformation.

Skin fell to the ground.

The people had been efficient accomplices to the skinning of their faces, to the unusual ritual of their disinheritance. They were skinned like goats before a ritual conceived to bring back the dead, that is, with happy song. They had lain in rows in the searing sun while their skin fell from their faces, pulled and pulled away. It was clear that is how the process had been executed, for their faces were perpetually astonished. It is like that with skins that are put out to dry. The people walked the streets without any faces, invisible, like ghosts. Was it a surprise then that they could not recognize one another? Ancestors dared not recognize them. The people had found such a breath-stopping freedom the ancestors knew them not, dared not know them. Faces dried under troubled rays. The people stopped in amazement, greeted each other, swept on. On the other side of the streets their skins burned an ill and silenced song. The streets smelled of burning skin. *Nyore Nyore.* It was like that in 1977.

～

eight

The silence cleansed her.

Mazvita gathered the whispering he had spread between her legs, over her arms, over her face. She ran far into the mist but the whispering, a frightful memory, encompassed her. She gathered the whispering into a silence that she held tightly within her body. She sheltered in the silence. The silence was hers, though he had initiated it. The silence was a quietness in her body, a deafness to the whispering that escaped from the lips of the stranger. He had claimed her, told her that she could not hide the things of her body, that she must bring a calabash of water within her arms, and he would drink. He had tired of drinking from the river. She must offer him water with cupped hands. She must kneel so that he could drink. He whispered as though he offered her life, in gentle murmuring tones, unhurried, but she felt his arms linger too long over her thighs, linger searchingly and cruelly, and she knew that if there was life offered between them, it was from herself to him—not offered, but taken.

The silence was a treasure. Mazvita felt a quietness creep from the earth into her body as he rested above her, spreading his whispered longing over her. She had slept very still, but briefly, before she started to run. She ran with the slipperiness pouring between her thighs, except she was not aware that her legs were still hers. She was aware, simply, that somewhere her skin carried a terrible wetness that she needed to defeat. Mazvita longed for a silence without a ripple or an echo in it.

He reached for her back and she lay motionless, unaware that she still had a name that was hers. She had discovered the silence to keep his breathing from her back. *Hanzvadzi* . . . he said. You are my sister . . . he whispered. He did not shout or raise his voice but invited her to lie still in a hushed but serious rhythm. His voice was monotonous, low, but firmly held in his mouth, in his arms. He spoke in a tone trained to be understood, not heard. Mazvita fought to silence his whispering. The task nearly killed her. It was difficult to find all his whispered words. She could not always recognize all the words, and when she did, her effort was to quickly gather them into that distance she had prepared inside of her. She longed deeply for the silence to be complete. She longed to escape the insistent cries of his triumph.

The silence was not a forgetting, but a beginning. She would grow from the silence he had brought to her. Her longing for growth was deep, and came from the parts of her body he had claimed for himself, which he had claimed against all her resistance and her tears. So she held her body tight to close him out, to keep the parts of her body that still belonged to her, to keep them near to herself, recognizable and near. She allowed her arms to move forward, ahead of her, and she ran through the mist, following her arms. She welcomed the stillness the silence brought to her body. It made her thoughts coherent, brought calm to her face. Mazvita was strong.

The tightness brought to her a complete silence, of her womanhood. She fought hard for the silence long after that morning. The days grew into months. The moon glowed a thin but silent awaiting. Mazvita had lost her seasons of motherhood. She did not question this dryness of her body but welcomed it as a beginning, a clear focus of her emotion, a protecting impulse. She was pure and strong and whole. She recovered her name. Mazvita. She sheltered in the barrenness and the silence of her name. She had discovered a redeeming silence. Mazvita.

Mazvita accepted the season of emptiness as her own particular fate. She grew from the emptiness. The emptiness lifted her from the ground and she felt something like power, like joy, move through her. The heaviness lifted from her shoulders and her arms, from her eyes which she had closed after the mist had collapsed into her eyes. Mazvita wished for an emotion as perfectly shaped as hate, harmful as sorrow, but she had not seen the man's face. She could not find his face, bring it close enough to attach this emotion to it. Hate required a face against which it could be flung but searching for the face was futile. Instead, she transferred the hate to the moment itself, to the morning, to the land, to the dew-covered grass that she had felt graze tenderly against her naked elbow in that horrible moment of his approach, transferred it to the prolonged forlorn call of the strange bird she heard cry a shrill cry in the distance, so shrill and loud that she had had to suppress her own cry which had risen to her lips. The unknown bird had silenced her when she needed to tell of her own suffering, to tell not to someone else—certainly not to the man—but to hear her own suffering uttered, acknowledged, within that unalterable encounter. A cry, her own cry, would have been a release of all the things she had lost. But she did not cry then and so it was as if she had lost the world. And all the many things that contained this loss continued to remind her of her pain. She transferred the hate to the something that she could see, that had shape and color and distance. The mist had taught her that morning is not always birth.

Mazvita felt the man breathe eagerly above her. She hated the breathing; she hated even more the longing in the breathing; mostly, she hated the land that pressed beneath her back as the man moved impatiently above her, into her, past her. Mazvita sought the emptiness of her body. Afterward, she did not connect this emptiness to the man because she thought of him not from inside her, but from outside. He had never been inside her. She connected him only to the land. It was the land that had come toward her. He had grown from the land. She saw him grow from the land, from the mist, from the river. The land had allowed the man to grow from itself into her body.

Mazvita gathered the silence from the land into her body.

~

"The land belongs to our feet because only they can carry the land. It is only our feet which own the land. Our hands can only carry clods of earth at a time. We cannot carry the land on our shoulders. No one can take the land away. To move away from the land is to admit that it has been taken. It is to abandon it. We have to wait here. We have to wait here with the land, if we are to be loyal to it, and to those who have given it to us. The land does not belong to us. We keep the land for the departed. That is why we can work on the land while strangers believe it can belong only to them. How can something so vast and mysterious belong to anybody? Only that which we can carry between our fingers can belong to us. No one can own the land. Because this is true we are fighting the strangers so that they leave, and we can protect the land. They have told us it is not right for us to protect the land, yet they have asked us to work on it. Have you seen them working on the land as we do? They are strangers to the land. Our feet own the land much more than the claims of their mouths, much more than the claims of their fingers. The land recognizes only those who work upon it. It knows our breath and our sweat."

Nyenyedzi spoke with a brightness on his face, a glow unhidden. He would not leave the land. But Mazvita did not agree with the vision he held for the land. She had no fear of departures. She was restless, though she admired and cared for this man. She turned away from him. She held a heaviness in her mouth that Nyenyedzi failed to fathom.

"We are servants paid poorly for our labors. We cannot decide which crop to grow, or when to grow it. We do not pray for the success of our crop because it is no longer our crop. We cannot pray for another's crop. There are no rituals of harvest, of planting the crop into the ground. We labor because it is our task to labor. We do not own the land. The land is enclosed in barbed fences, and we sleep amid the thornbushes, in the barren part of the land. We live in fear because even those who fight in our name threaten our lives.

"It is like that with a war. We must remain here or else join the fight, fight to cleanse the land, not find new dreams to replace our ancient claim.

"The land has forgotten us. Perhaps it dreams new dreams for itself.

"You lack patience and hope, Mazvita, you want things to belong to you, just like the stranger does. You want to possess, to hold things between your hands and say they belong to you. You do not see that things belong to you not because you have held them, but because they have held you. It is like that with the land. It holds and claims you. The land is inescapable. It is everything. Without the land there is no day or night, there is no dream. The land defines our unities. There is no prayer that reaches our ancestors without blessing from the land. Land is birth and death. If we agree that the land has forgotten us, then we agree to be dead."

"What you say about the land is true, but does this truth belong equally to all of us?"

"The truth does not belong to anyone. It is our truth."

"Truth changes like a sky. The strangers have taken the land. They have grown tobacco where we once buried the dead. The dead remain silent. They have grown tobacco where we once worshipped and prayed. The land has not rejected them. They have harvested much crop. I remember . . ."

"They have not grown the crop. We have grown the crop. The land has yielded to our hand. They will leave the land. We are fighting them."

"We wait . . . we wait for a new death . . . for the death of the land."

"The land has claimed us for its truth."

"I remember . . ."

Mazvita understood that Nyenyedzi would not agree to leave, that he would wait here, or else join the fight. Either way he did not belong to her. She wanted something different for her truth. She wanted to conquer her reality then, and not endure the suspension of time. She felt a strong sense of her own power and authority, of her ability to influence and change definitions of her own reality, adjust boundaries to her vision, banish limits to her progress. She felt supreme with every moment. She had left Mubaira because it suited her to move forward. She possessed a strong desire for her liberty, and did not want to linger hopelessly between one vision and the next. She had loved the land, saw it through passionate and intense moments of freedom, but to her the land had no fixed loyalties. She gathered from it her freedom which it delivered to her wholly and specially. If it yielded crop, then it could also free her, like the plants which grew upon it and let off their own blooms, their own scents, their own color, while anchored on the land. She felt free like a seed released from one of such plants. She could grow anywhere. Mazvita felt buoyant. Her relationship to the land involved such buoyant freedoms. She had the potential to begin again. Hope mingled with desire. Mazvita was ambitious. She wanted to discover something new in her world. She understood the kind of loyalty Nyenyedzi referred to, but she was ready to move into another sphere of presence, to depart. She did not care for certainties, each moment would uncover its secret, but she would be there, ahead of that moment, far ahead. She moved close to Nyenyedzi, and touched him. Mazvita had no fear of departures.

～

A violent wind carried Mazvita forward.

No one noticed or remembered her. Mazvita was sure of her direction so she started to walk. Her footsteps were jerky and faltering. She walked. She walked sideways, because her left shoulder leaned forward. It was her broken side. Her bones spread in splintered fragments, across her back. She leaned farther sideways and felt, once more, her bones fall against each other. Her bones built a mountain on her back.

Mazvita. Her back was broken.

It was hard to support the child when her back was so much broken, but she tried, and she tried to walk quickly through the crowds. It was hard work. Harare was busy and indifferent.

Mazvita. Her eyes were unseeing. They simply led her forward. She had surrendered her sight when she heard the violent breaking on her back. She had relieved herself of sight because it was easier to be blind and still journey forward. She had surrendered her own eyes because it suited her to do so. The ritual was fulfilling and complete. She lost all capacity for dream. She felt less burdened, less susceptible to injury. After all she had injured herself irreparably, she could not hurt beyond the hurting so hurtful. Empty and abandoned, she walked, leaning forward, past caring.

The city pushed forward. It was 1977. It was nothing to see a woman with a blind stare on her face, with a baby fixed spidery on her back. It was nothing to be sorrowful. The city was like that. There was a uniformity about suffering, a wisdom about securing your own kind of suffering, your own version of going forward. The idea was to go forward, even those who had died in the streets knew that, they crawled toward the alleys.

Death, properly executed, could be mistaken for progress.

~

eleven

Cloth ripped downward, and the children ran with naked shoulders toward their mothers. They crept beneath the barbed wire and rose from the ground to nurse their bruised ankles.

The building sat in a mud row on the edge of the barbed wire. Two parallel walls of mud and poles had been built then subdivided to form tight cramped residences for the workers. On one side low entrances were carved into the wall. The place was grass-thatched. The grass hung low behind the huts, left gaps that allowed the smoke to escape, allowed the sun to enter freely, allowed the rain. Often the men retrieved wide plastic bags once used to cover the tobacco when it was carried to the city, and they tied these over the holes. The thatching was made of intermittent marriages of plastic and grass. A row could contain up to six dwellings. There was no land granted to build well-spaced huts.

From the entrance, which was black with smoke, Nyenyedzi watched Mazvita kneel beside the fire preparing the evening meal. She felt him standing there because the slice of light which had been illuminating the room had vanished. He remained quiet. He entered in slow guarded footsteps and sat at the opposite side of the fire.

"Can I get more wood for you?" he asked. His asking was richly coated, longing. The bag she had already packed was hidden in the recesses of the room, pushed under the blankets folded among the utensils, among the things they had shared, before sharing this. She felt their heavy parting. She blew hard at the fire, and paused. She held her breath as it moved upward. She held her breath there where her chest was pushed outward. She held the moment of their sharing in her mouth. She paused. She released her breath, gathered softly, from her mouth, from deep in her stomach. Her head dropped down.

"I did not see that you had arrived. The food is almost ready." She rose, turned backward, retrieved a vessel filled with water. Nyenyedzi rose, bent beneath the doorway, passed through, then stood outside. He waited for her.

She followed Nyenyedzi with the water in the basin. He held both hands out and she poured the water over him. He rubbed his hands together, and washed them. She paused as he rubbed the dirt from his fingers. She watched him dig beneath his nails, search deep into the crevices. His nails were wide and flat and cracked, black with the soil. He held out his hands and she poured the water over them. The water fell to the ground, splashed onto her bare feet. She allowed the water to descend, gently, over his hands.

She handed him the basin, now half full with the water, and he poured the water over her hands. She washed her hands rapidly and nervously. He poured the water very deliberately over her hands. She grew anxious through his pleading. The water fell over her bare arms and ran over the back of her hands. She turned her hands and received the water which brought the setting sun in drops to her fingers. She extended her arms and held her hands away from her body. She washed her hands and thanked him. She retrieved the basin from him, empty, and turned to enter the unlit room that they had shared. He followed cautiously behind her. The fire was dying.

"Mazvita," he called, as she entered. She stood still. She could hardly bear it. The stillness was theirs. It was heavy.

"The land . . . we cannot forget it, it cannot forget us," Nyenyedzi muttered.

She served the food and they ate, held in silence, in their fears, their desires. He pleaded.

Mazvita fought with each gesture of her hand, with her eyebrows raised and searching, with her feet held beneath her body, shoulders raised, a forehead tired and wet, toes patiently curled, her back leaning away from him.

He held a pleading desperate gaze. He called upon the land to give to him this woman that he cared for. He could not leave the land, and be a man. He was afraid of returning and not knowing the land, of the land not knowing him. He feared untried absences. He preferred the histories of his people.

The woman rose above the land and scorned its slow promises, its intermittent loyalties. She had such a will, and he knew that he could not equal her passion for beginnings. He heard her fight, heard her defeat him, in that silence. He raised his head from the plate of food, and met her. The woman confronted the land with her passion for escape.

"Mazvita," he called.

Mazvita carried a bold frantic gaze that Nyenyedzi failed to recognize.

They were free, finally, of each other's desires.

≈

t w e l v e

Mazvita could no longer remember the woman who had sold her the apron. *Amai.* She remembered that. *Amai.* She was indeed a mother. It was heavy to be a mother. It made one recognizable in the streets, even when one no longer recognized oneself. *Amai.* It was painful. *Amai.* The seller's voice followed her through the crowds, but it no longer referred to her. *Amai.* It referred to any woman who passed by, who carried a baby on her back, who was a potential mother. *Amai.* It had never referred to her, that *Amai*, at least not specifically. She had adopted the woman's voice for her truth. It was not enough. *Amai* referred only to her silver coins. Mazvita was alone.

The white apron spread across her back like a skinned animal. The baby rested within it, its head folded down. The head was heavy. Mazvita felt the head grow heavy on her back. She wiped her face with a lonely naked arm, then spread her hands cupped to her back, circling the baby. Her hands met, joined, behind her back. Her palms grew warm. Mazvita buried the baby in her arms. Mazvita had tucked some of the baby's clothes along the sides of the apron where there were pockets of empty space, above the baby's knees where its legs attempted to curve around her waist. It was the two bottom ends of the apron that she felt cut through her waist. She had gathered the endless lengths of stitched apron bands and tied them firmly. She had tied the bands to fight the weight of the child. Mazvita buried the baby on her back.

Mazvita repeatedly formed an incredibly tight knot, then a short while later she would untie the bands, and start all over again, convinced that the knot was not firm enough, that the baby might fall out, that someone might pause long enough to look into her secret. She harnessed all her strength, all her memories. Each grew threateningly faint. Untying the bands was not easy, but she fought the knot. She bit dangerously, her neck pulled forward, her shoulders peaks of anguish.

Mazvita was in a fierce protracted battle with the apron, tying it, untying it, tying it. With each secured moment of her untying, she bent her back forward, leaned toward the ground, and felt the baby slide forward toward her neck, slide forward. A silent sliding, and her neck shrunk with cold. Her head fell backward, toward the baby.

Her head met that of the baby in a soft loving collision. It was growing soft that head pressed on her back. Soft. She panicked at the thought but the thought pressed hard beneath her armpits, and she felt a sweat break freely there, flow in ripples of salty tears. The air was stale and hot, it was not to be trusted, and the baby was so heavily wrapped. The air hung over the ears with a promise of fatality.

She touched what she thought was the baby's forehead with the back of her head, and felt consoled. The baby felt hard. Her knees trem-

bled and sank downward. Mazvita. She remembered at least her own
name and sang it to her baby. She sang deep and slow. She sang deep
deep, from her insides to her baby, a lullaby that came from the recesses
of an ancient memory. The tune was familiar, but coarse, it seemed
ground from between two violent stones. It was a tune for grinding
corn, not for awakening tenderness. Mazvita, she sang. She polished her
song into a rhythmic but futile undertaking. She sang with arms spread
wide in a spontaneous greeting of the earth, a weeping farewell. Her
arms were heavy with the child, remembered. She spread her arms wide
like the sky.

It was a song lyrical and free. She sent a song from her back to the
waiting child, fed the baby with that song, with her name. The song was
the only thing that belonged to her and that she could still remember,
that made any kind of sense to her, for the future held her fate in disarray. She could offer the song. She was desperate and lost. A song was a
kind of freedom, a promise of birth and beginnings. Dear was that name
she fed to her child, a ululating symphony, a melody enchanting and
lonesome. She sang with the last breath in her body, for she was certain
there would be no life for her after this. It was not possible that she
would be buried and then live. She had died a final death.

Mazvita did not know if she was going to Mubaira or Kadoma. Both
destinations seemed necessary and certain. She had arrived here. She
had arrived there. She knew nothing of arrivals, only departures. She
knew about departures because she had mistaken them for beginnings.
Departures were not beginnings, they were resolutions, perhaps, they
were acts of courage, perhaps. Futile illusions had marked her departures. Birth, for her, had not been a beginning, but a newer kind of departure, an entrapment rare and nullifying. She had tired of departures.
Mazvita tried to imagine that there was a beginning even in this sorrowful finality. It seemed the end had always been there, had always waited.

She could decide on the bus, about her destination. It did not matter, because the destination was only another place in her journey. She saw herself unanchored, moving forward, always moving forward, with the weight of the baby on her back. She would never rid herself of this particular suffering. The baby was her own, truly her own burden. Now her main concern was to secure a seat on the bus. A part of her said there were beginnings, in both directions. She had a rare chance to choose her beginnings, to undo her past. She might choose the point of birth, or of love. There were inviting dramas in both, passions bright and elegant. She had begun twice in her life, perhaps three times, perhaps such a number of times there was really no use counting, for what was it to begin?

Mazvita knew about waterfalls because she had found herself on the edge of a cliff. She had not known there were such rugged and desperate spaces in which one could continue to live, even though a massive river tumbled over one's head, and stones followed, and boulders beat against the shoulders, and one screamed and screamed. One could live in such uninhabitable places.

Mazvita felt herself tumble and fall but there was no ground beneath, only an interminable echo which she followed with her body while it spiraled into a darkness loud and indifferent. She had not fallen like that, because she held herself against the hard ground, pushed her right palm down, and rose awkwardly. She steadied herself, and moved on. She still heard the echo that she had followed, and mistrusted it. One side of her arm, on which she had fallen, was covered in dust. Her face was bruised. She passed a dry tongue over her cracked upper lip. There were parts of herself she dared not trust. The truths her imagination asserted formed a major part of her distrust, of her hopelessness. She trusted only the cold weight on her back—the toes small, curled and cold. She straightened her back. She stood still.

Mazvita held on to the baby and the apron and the last strands of sanity, to propel her steadily forward, for she carried such a weight on her back. She untied the apron string once more, cautiously but quickly. And as usual, she cast a loud searching glance toward her surroundings. The baby was precious, not like jewels, but like hope finely chiseled. It was like that with the baby.

She untied the apron. She looked frantically around. The pain tore at her back. The betrayal was familiar, so she ignored it and went on with her task. Her fingers had mastered an unimaginable dexterity, proportionate to her suffering. Without lifting her head she turned her eyes stealthily to the left, stealthily to the right, then closed them in one unhesitating movement. A scream threatened to escape from her throat. Her throat was constricted and yet she felt the scream push like a current upward toward her mouth. She held her eyes tightly closed.

She leaned forward and felt the apron grow loose over her shoulders. It cut her shoulders, the apron. It pierced the place where her arm swung forward, backward. Her arm swung forward ever so loosely, like wet bark hanging on the side of a trunk, freshly peeled. She was surprised that she could still manipulate her arm, bring it forward, pull that last bit of strength from it and transfer it to the knot forming on the apron. How was she to undo that knot but to lie down, and die.

She had lost her freedom. Death was another kind of freedom, and she longed for it. Her death, that is.

She protected a longing deep as death.

∾

t h i r t e e n

Mazvita did not have to know anyone. Not herself, not anyone. Knowing was a hindrance. It pinned you down. After that
you started recognizing people. Recognizing yourself. That was
the danger. It was best to remain anonymous. Some things you
just can't figure out. Harare was like that. To be here was not to be
here at all, that's what made being here. It was special. The absence
filled you up. It didn't creep up on you, try to surprise you, gently
and anonymously. You walked right into it, hard like a wall. Hard
hitting hardness. Concrete and rock hit you on the forehead and if
you were lucky it broke your skull, then there was nothing to remember, the absence was total. A new life began, grew around
you, embraced you like a hurricane. Sometimes it killed you. That
was what was good about absence. Its dependability. Its un-

doubted ability for harm. People liked that about absence. They had tired of being here, choking on every thought. Thinking was dangerous. Absence more so. They chose the greater danger, arriving unprotected, ready to be injured. That is how naive they were about freedom.

Freedom was round and smooth and yellow, an earthly version of the sun, handheld. But who ever heard of a handheld freedom? Yet each sought an egg laid with only them in mind, laid right into their palm, warm, wet, soft.

It was like that when she arrived in the city. She felt a rare freedom eagerly anticipated. It moved over her just like that. The buildings were so high they made her want to crouch, or bury herself in the ground, anything but to walk up straight. She collapsed in a heap on the pavement and watched the cars move past. She sat curled on the cold cement block. Multitudes of feet moved by. Harare was a pestilence. Feet swished past. The city was unapologetic. The city was on time. Harare was festive. Roads were four-wheeled, black-tarred and moving.

No one cast her a pitiful glance. She was not there at all. Her name was only hers, she could change it at any time. She called herself Rosie while she sat there, and laughed inwardly. She called herself Mildred . . . then Margaret . . . then Angelina . . . then Constance . . . Juliet. She preferred Julie to Juliet. Mazvita, she would remain. She did not want to remember what Nyenyedzi had called her. A name like that was not for remembering in the midst of such drumming. The city was busy in every direction that she looked, and she looked everywhere.

It was a rare kind of freedom this, to be so busy and purposeful. She wondered what happened to the aged, in this city so determined to be free, for the old tempered movement, tempered dream. The city was a place which hid its old. Perhaps no one ever lived here long enough to be toothless. If you had no teeth here, you had no life. That much was clear. It never occurred to her that the young also died natural deaths.

Feet moved in whirls of free-flowing cloth. Men and women wore trousers. REVOLUTION—a small tag along the waist, in black and white. The widened bottoms of the trousers turned and turned. It was also an era for turntables and long play. Freedom came in circles. Endless and dizzying. What was freedom if it could be curtailed and contained and passed around? Freedom was a thought tantalizing and personal. You had to wear your own freedom to be sure it had arrived. 1977. That is how it was expressed. People walked into shops and bought revolutions. If your revolution was white, and wide, then you had circled your dream, made a complete revolution more definite than the sun. There was a satellite to every vision. It was not a year for comets, really, though fire colored the sky. That fire was the periphery of dream, not the dream itself. The dream was physical, a caress. It circled ankles. Clad into an expanding silhouette, you died in the streets and it did not matter. You could starve to death. Everyone was an overclad and spearless revolutionary. Magazines showed former slaves with a new gospel of truth and freedom. But here they had not inherited the blood of foraging white masters and therefore worked extra hard to achieve that fine Afro hair. Men heated metal, close-toothed Afro combs and lifted their hair from the scalp; the women, who already knew freedom was purchasable, walked into glittering *Ambi* shops and bought their prepared Afro wigs. Thus clad, they asserted an inchoate independence. Independence was memory and style. Black had never been as beautiful as when it married slavery with freedom.

~

f o u r t e e n

There were no greetings, preliminaries, or rituals to courtship. At least none that Mazvita recognized. The man walked up to
her in easy loitering footsteps on the side of the road where she
sat. He swung efficiently toward her. She noticed his arm swing
forward. He swung his arms in obvious and deliberate motions of
liberty. He did not keep still even as he asked her if she needed a
place to stay. He had such a look . . . It suited her to consider he
was being thoroughly helpful. That is how naive she was about his
freedom.

He was tall, and when he spoke, his voice departed in sudden hissing spurts. His face was round and small, and his
mouth was wide. His mouth seemed unsuited to his small

face. His teeth were set evenly beneath a small nose. He swung his arm repeatedly toward his nose, and wiped it down. He swung his right arm like this between every sentence, in between his arm hung as if helpless. The gesture made him sympathetic. It was not clear whether he had acquired the gesture to draw attention to his nose or to hide it. It was the same with his legs. They were thin and long and swung forward with each movement. It was possible he had thought of swinging his right leg to wipe his nose. Mazvita stared at him in fascination.

He offered to take her home on his bicycle, his fingers swinging, pointing, from his wrist at the bicycle which waited on the opposite side of the road. He pulled his head toward her, toward the bicycle, back to her. The decision was easy.

Mazvita had never sat on a bicycle before. The thought made her strange, eager, and careless. It tantalized her. It seemed inevitable that she should start life in the city with an elaborate undertaking. They moved together toward the bicycle. He swung determinedly ahead. He searched backward to ensure that she followed. His head made a quick backward glance, swept forward. She watched his newness with a fascinated stare. She held her head carefully above her shoulders. The cars screeched to a stop, moved on, screeched again.

He made her sit with both her legs to one side of the road, and when he turned, she had to pull her weight back to regain her support. The whole exercise was free, pleasurable, careless, and uncaring. A public display. She was so involved with her particular version of freedom she did not see that no one noticed her. Ornate yellow blooms kept her memory hopeful. Then she turned a corner and met another woman sitting just like her, and she wanted to wave at their mutual freedom. But she needed both hands to hold on to the seat if she was to remain stable, so she hesitated, and in any case, when she looked at the woman, there was no sign of recognition or sharing.

The man took little time to know her. He was agile.

"Joel. I am Joel." He cast a searching hesitating glance at her, then turned to look in the distance.

"Mazvita," she said warmly. She was getting used to this nimble creature. His mouth was wide. She expected him to make elaborate declarations. He was quick with his mouth, with all his moves. Joel.

Joel liked this new girl. She was shy and self-possessed. She would not ask him for money like all those other girls he had gone through. If he had anything to do with it he would keep her here. At least till he tired of her.

Joel was a miracle. He rode through many streets, oblivious of the hooters. He had a quickness in his speech, a quickness in his movements, a quickness everywhere. She did not find these habits suspicious. She simply stared at his quick legs and fingers. His eyes blinked so quickly that it was a miracle he saw anything. Nyenyedzi was not quick like that. The idea of thinking of this man and of Nyenyedzi at the same time made her laugh. This man was like a machine, ready to go somewhere. She wondered if all the men in the city were like this. He did not even ask to touch her but simply took off his clothes, dropped them on the floor, lay down beside her. "Sleep . . . sleep," he said afterward. He was brief. That is how their life together began. There was no discussion, no agreement, no proposal. They just met and stayed together.

It was strange, but it was a freedom divine. Rituals can be inhibiting. Instead, they had a limitless potential to dream, to travel anywhere, if it had occurred to them. In truth, they really could not put the potential to much use. Still, they had a potential and they had claimed it for their truth. Rituals were not livable in Harare, so they forgot about them and created empty spaces in which they wandered aimlessly. It was a torture sometimes, to have so little to care for, but the emptiness was theirs, and it was authentic.

Joel never spoke of consulting her parents concerning living with her like this. Mazvita found herself wondering about it. Though she had told herself this was freedom, it was not easy to forget where she had come from. They lived as though they had no pasts or futures. They lived because they found themselves living, because one was a man, the other a woman, and it was in their nature to need each other. There were no apologies for such spontaneous needs. There were no resolutions or recollections. The present was brimming with ecstasy, with silhouettes of dream. There were no obstacles to their reality. They settled into a life together, in which Joel leapt out of bed in the morning, leapt back in at night. She adjusted to his rhythm. She liked him. He had made Harare easy and reachable for her.

Joel woke in the mist of morning. He never told her where he worked. It was an unnecessary detail. Details were cumbersome. So they stumbled over them, and moved on. They shoved them aside, hid them, burned them, anything but disclosed them. It was better to maintain the strangeness, it kept everything fresh and exciting. Details meant communicating and intimacy. The main point of freedom was maintaining boundaries, though such boundaries were questionable. Mazvita and Joel simply lived together, kept their pasts from each other. It did not matter where they had come from. It did not concern them who had brought them into the world. The city was cramped with discordant sound.

Mazvita became an efficient housekeeper. She ironed Joel's white shirts till they shone. Joel sat on the small bed on weekends in a crisp shirt and paged through *Scope* magazine. Half-naked white women graced the covers of *Scope*, in tight bikinis. Joel read torn and soiled copies of James Hadley Chase, and grinned marvelously. One day he read a copy of *The Way the Cookie Crumbles* and made love to her on the floor. It was so very quick. She wondered what was in that Hadley Chase. He held her head in the crook of his arm, and read.

≈

fifteen

The bus was full of people. They jostled and found seats on which to settle and exchange greetings. Greetings that were mere affirmations of direction.

"Are you going to Mubaira?"

"Yes, I am going to Mubaira, and you?"

"Yes. I am going to Mubaira. My wife is waiting for me there. It is our home because my wife is there. She plants the crops."

"I work in the city too. My wife also plants the crops. The city is only for the money we get. I cannot let my wife join me. The city is corrupt. A serious woman will not manage to live there. A woman can lose her head. Only a man can manage those streets, those lights, those policemen. It is terrible there. If you marry a woman from the city you will have made a fire and sat on it. She will even tell you to cook. She will ask you to help unbutton her bra. What kind of a thing is that? I prefer a woman whose breasts are free and waiting. Take me home now . . . the women say to a man who is passing by . . . the women swing with their hips, swing arms covered in plastic bangles. Women's legs are nylon and high. Heels do not touch the ground. Handbags swing across arms, cross the streets. 1977. There is a scorpion beneath every rock. The city makes a man frenzied and hot. The freedom in that city! My wife stays at home, we had a large harvest of groundnuts last year. A whole ten sacks. I wonder how she did it, but a woman's strength is not to be frowned upon."

"It is not the woman. It is the rain. There was a lot of rain last year. All the women had to do was merely harvest."

"Harvesting is work."

"Yes. It is a woman's work. A woman's back is strong. A man cannot bend like that all day. A man cannot bend like a woman."

"And carry a baby on her back too. A woman's back is made for work. A woman's back is strong as stone."

"The bus is full. It is such a hot day. I don't know if it will rain this year as it did last year. The earth has changed. Who ever heard of such heat? A heat like this brings death."

"Such heat brings rain. It never comes alone. It brings good crops. When the earth is thirsty like this, the rain finally falls in torrents. It shall rain so much we must make ready the thatching of our huts or we shall be left sitting in a clearing."

"A woman's back can perform miracles. We had such a large harvest of groundnuts. Then there was the maize, I cannot even begin to tell you about that. The maize filled four large granaries. If the rain does not fall this year, we shall be safe for another three years, at least."

"We harvested a lot too. But I am certain this heat means rain. I plan to sell all the harvested crop and buy a plow, then we shall really prepare the fields for a harvest to humble all harvests. I am certain of it. This heat brings rain."

The conductor ducked between the many heads, between the two men who shared a seat and talked. The conductor ducked among the heads clad in shining bright scarves which were tied in small loose knots at the back of the women's heads. The scarves were damp along the edges, and carried large smudges of wetness at the top. It was hot on the bus. The women had freed their babies from the back and held them. Most of the babies slept.

The conductor handed tickets out, received some money. He carried a black leather bag bound tightly around his waist, it bounced with his every agile movement. He was rather like an excited locust lost in tall grasses. He could ferret out a passenger who had not paid, without any effort at all. He held his nose pinched into a mole which he kept safe between his eyes, then he turned his head sideways, very quickly. The leather purse was a constant reminder of his importance. His forehead hid beneath a massive fall of thick black hair. He pulled his arm back, shoved it into his leather purse, picked out several coins, leapt forward. His neck jerked sideways. He darted past Mazvita, though she had not paid.

Mazvita saw him move past her. She watched him disappear among the mounds of tied boxes blocking the path to the back. He surfaced, beyond the obstructions, over the large box tightly tied with a black elastic band.

≈

sixteen

Mazvita arrived in Harare ready to claim her freedom. Here, she was protected from the hills and the land. Harare banished memory, encouraged hope. Mazvita had a strong desire to grow. She trusted the future and her growth and her desire. She had faith in untried realities because she trusted her own power for change, for adaptation. She welcomed each day with a strong sense of her desire, of her ability to begin, of her belonging. Mazvita had a profound belief in her own reality, in the transformation new geographies promised and allowed, that Harare's particular strangeness released and encouraged. Mazvita recognized Harare as the limitless place in which to dream, and to escape.

Mazvita drew on her own capacity for release which had led her here. She was not frivolous in her ambition. She hoped only not to be harmed by the compromises she had found unavoidable. Joel was inevitable in her existence.

Mazvita was oppressed by her desire for time. She knew that this awareness did not coincide with Harare as she encountered it. Harare challenged the demarcations between day and night, offered distances from time, for part of being here was the forgetting of boundaries to days, of challenging futures. In Harare, years could go by and it would be as though one had arrived only yesterday. The discoveries offered by the city were tempting and endless . . . The city was contemptuous, it asked, did you only arrive yesterday? Sleep and slowness were denied to those who were of the city. There was no room for sleep because one day led into another without pause, and when you had been in it long enough, you did not make the kind of mistakes that exposed your failure to flow with its time. However, what was it to be here long enough when truly there was no clear measure of time?

Time was precious. Mazvita was caught up in this whirl of time, of freed existence, yet those first days with Joel still weighed heavy on her, because she needed time to secure her freedom. She felt that each day she was without employment drew her closer to Joel and emphasized her dependability. She hoped to recover the time she had spent with Joel because she needed it for herself, for her own growth. She did not share in the belief that time was continuous and endless, that what she had not accomplished today was easily recoverable. She had not banished the future in the way that people in the city had done. It made her frantic and restless to think of the future.

She felt tired, as though she fought against a strong current that determined to move against her. The future threatened her, it was large. She did not want to fall emptily into the future. She did not want to be surprised by it, so she worked hard to prepare for each moment before the moment found her. She hid when she could. Time moved on and drew her from her hiding. Mazvita longed for a future in which she would look backward and feel fulfillment, so her divisions of time were cautious and labored.

She hoped to succeed. Success could only be measured by holding the past against the future. While Harare set a pace for her existence Mazvita located herself beyond the moment. Mazvita had tired of postponements to her vision. She tried to understand the ceaseless yet inviting ambivalences that defined the city. Mazvita weighed carefully the city's offerings and denials, its testimonies and silences.

At night yellow and white lights mingled and burned and the sight spread, in the distance, a prophecy of their liberation. It did not matter that they lived in the darkness, with no such lights. It mattered only that they lived close to this spectacular vision, to this vibrating light. The city proposed luminous aspirations. Mazvita felt immediately that there was something to be hoped for in this nearness to the city. Fear attached to her arrival, but the fear was exciting, because it offered release. Mazvita allowed herself to hope. Joel was only another version of the city, an aspect of her potential freedom.

She had met Joel. She liked Joel. She lived with Joel. Joel was not Nyenyedzi, and she had left Nyenyedzi. She did not dream dreams around Joel. She dreamt dreams around herself. In Harare, however, Joel was necessary to her dream. Part of her Harare was Joel. Joel made Harare accessible. The city included Joel.

Mazvita knew that Joel was part of a definition of Harare that she had not anticipated. She had not anticipated the city in its entirety. There were more compromises to be made than she had thought. She looked for work while Joel was away. Mazvita quickly saw that Joel had his own version of the city, and that he was weaving her into it. She would not succumb to being a mere aspect of his dream.

Mazvita was free of Joel. She had sought her dream first, ahead of him, and it was not possible that she would fail because of his particular instinct of dream. She allowed Joel to believe that she had no plans for the future. The deception was easy to accomplish; after all, in Harare the future was considered present and urgent. It suited Joel to believe that, to Mazvita, he was an unmistakable version of the future.

First she looked for work in all the wrong places, then she learned that the most immediate work she could secure was not in the smoke-filled industrial areas, but in the affluent homes located on the other side of the hills, behind that yellow horizon she met every evening. Mazvita was definite that she had not come to the city simply to nurse the children of strangers. She would look for another kind of employment. She waited. She thought very hard of the employment she would have liked to secure. She dreamt of herself freed from Joel. She did not like to ask for money and felt uncomfortable when she had to. It was enough that she stayed in Joel's room and ate the food he bought. Joel offered her respite while she searched hard for work. Mainly, she searched for who she was, as she had realized that in the city she was someone new and different, someone she had not met. Mazvita had to find her Harare. She had to find a voice with which to speak, without trying to hide from herself. She had to look up when someone spoke to her or else her newness betrayed her. She had to laugh with more abandon, not with the restraint she had brought from Mubaira, and to walk too with firmer footsteps. Mazvita felt that freedom was here, but hidden to her. She had to find work first, then perhaps she might feel the release that she wished. She might even leave Joel, or if she stayed with him, it would be with the knowledge that she could leave when she desired it.

Mazvita hoped desperately to find a job in the city.

～

seventeen

Joel stirred her abandoned cry.

Mazvita was completely alone while she was with Joel. She closed her eyes and heard him move quickly above her. His movements were erratic as he sought her between the torn covers. A thin light sifted through the worn curtains and caught her arm over his head, in the darkness. She did not see the light. Her eyes were closed. Joel saw her eyes close and imagined the closing was about him, about his fingers touching her face, touching the curve of her eyes, searching her forehead. But Mazvita was alone. She imagined Joel was alone too. There were no words spoken between them.

Through the mist Mazvita smelled the stale gray blankets, the worn-out mattress, heard the bell of a bicycle ring below the window, sewage water flowing across obstacles through a ditch beside the road, a man shouting angrily at a barking dog, a stone hitting one side of the wall.

Mazvita tried not to remember Joel as he rested above her. She tried to be alone but she could not be apart from him if she carried his face along, so she chose to forget Joel's face. It was hard to forget Joel. Mazvita buried Joel in the mist. The burying was difficult because Joel would not keep still. Mazvita turned her face from Joel as he moved toward her. She turned her face downward to the pillow, but he turned her face back toward himself. He released her neck from his grasp. She closed her eyes tighter and waited. She waited till she felt him pull her legs toward him, till he rested almost still, over her. He was motionless and heavy above her. If she moved slightly he would begin to move again. He gathered his strength from her calm. She remained quiet to accommodate him. If she moved just then, he would turn away, cursing and telling her to be still. She must be still when he desired pause. She welcomed this brief moment when he rested in an undisturbed quiet. Then she cried.

He felt her tremble beneath him and shift her legs a little, away from him. She heard herself cry. She cried till only she could be heard. Joel interrupted her crying with his breathing. She felt him breathe. He did not speak but held her tighter toward himself. She did not feel his actions at all, though he truly held her tight. She heard only her cry, which expanded into the hollow spaces within her, into the silence she had conceived for herself, into the past of her memory. She lingered in her remembrance. The cry was a divine healing in which she stood alone, and whole. The cry was a triumph of her will, prolonged and full of her weeping, full of her laughter. She did not understand why she needed to laugh when the moment was so painful for her but she laughed in a breathless, broken spasm, in a distressful abandon. The laughter mixed with her tears. It was Joel she laughed at, she was sure. So when her laughing had struggled enough with her crying she reached her arms toward Joel and held him close to her breast till her tears fell downward past her temples and made the pillow wet. The mist fell from her eyes and she saw Joel's clothes that were pegged to the walls, saw Joel, fallen asleep.

Mubaira was so far away it vanished from memory. Mazvita remembered the cry she had heard above Joel's anxious breath, heard above the paraffin that spread in the room, the soot, above the darkness growing in the room, the roof, above herself. Mazvita listened above the whirls of days and months that separated her from Mubaira. But Mazvita did not understand that the cry had defeated the silence in her body, that the cry was a release dangerous and regrettable. The cry was not the lulling freedom she sought. After her discovery Mazvita would once again long that the solitude had protected her, long that the hollow spaces within her had remained hollow, the silence supreme.

❀

eighteen

The city women conjured freedom from chaos. They had red lips. Their carnival was new and persistent, for the women could be trusted to awaken the dead. The women proposed incredible assignations. They showed their capacity for absurdities, for building altars to wounded dreams. The vision they offered to the initiate was freeing and enticing. Prayers rose unsung from their lush lips. It was really not so hard to understand. The curious let the women pass in hordes, and stared at their threatening shoulders and their surprised eyebrows. The brave followed them in equally evocative disguises, carrying even stranger pronouncements on their faces. It was not clear whether the women sought speech or silence, peace or war, with such masks. There was an elaborate secret, no doubt, for the gesture itself was astounding. They chose red for the color of their fantastic realizations.

What uncommon deities were resurrected by the women! Red mud was spread beneath dreaming eyes. The carnival was barefaced and unbelievable, full of mimicry and death. The war was articulated in masks of dream and escape. It found expression in terror and courtship, in an excited sensuality, in figures speechless and dead. Guns soured the sky with black smoke.

The women picked their colors from a burning sun, from the lips of white women, then offered their bodies as a ransom for their land, their departed men, their corrupted rituals of birth. This bold and frantic gesture marked the ceremony for beginnings. In the silence that followed their transformation the women cried loud and clear and painted their nails a rhythmic red. The carnival was necessary and complete, so they lay in their dead bodies which they had rejected in the heightening clamor of the voices of their men, in the turmoil of fainthearted whispers.

The year was 1977.

～

Joel. A stirring, of nausea, circling and turning. Mazvita lay still on the bed. It was dark in the room. She lay still and tried to bury the child inside her body. Mazvita buried the child. She would keep the child inside her body, not give birth to it. Joel must not discover that her body had betrayed them like this.

Joel. She could not think about Joel and the pregnancy together. Joel definitely would not want to hear about it. They had not agreed on any kind of permanency. If she was pregnant, then it was best to keep the knowledge to herself.

She had not thought the right thoughts to keep this child away. How could she have conceived the child without some knowledge in the matter? It burdened her, this surreptitious birth. Mazvita rejected the baby because it pulled her back from her design to be free. Harare was cramped and relentless. She did not imagine where she would give birth in this chaos of voices, of dancing voices. Her stomach heaved into her mouth. She leaned over the bed and vomited into a dish resting on the side of the bed. Her eyes burned with bitter tears. She held the nausea in her mouth, deep into her body. The burning spread down her throat. She hoped the burning would stop so that she could think, make precise decisions.

Mazvita buried the child. Joel would never know a thing about it.

Joel. The idea of giving Joel a child made her laugh, though she felt miserable. He had made no promises to her. Joel could leave whenever he wanted. She could leave when she wanted. So far she wanted to stay. A child interfered with her decision to stay.

Mazvita crouched beside the bed and vomited into the basin. The pain tightened around her chest, twisted, and rested there. If she moved her body forward, she was sure the pain would be unbearable, so she held her hands close to her chest, and remained still. She kept the vomiting inside her chest. The pain coiled and fastened above her stomach. She writhed, turned, and leaned once more into the basin. Her nostrils filled with mucus and she pressed her face on the bed and wiped her nose on the coarse gray blanket. She pressed her face hard on the bed, her body held down. Her face itched from the blanket and her eyes watered. She sneezed and curled upward from the bed. She knelt with her face still pressed on the bed. Mazvita brought her forehead to her knees. She was curled stiffly on the bed. She grew silent. Mazvita buried the child in her body.

She carried the basin outside. She rinsed the basin, slowly and carefully, under the tap outside the toilet, her legs stiff and weak. She walked slowly, painfully, back into the house. She sank on the bed and coughed terribly. Her arms ached. Her forehead grew wet. Her arms trembled, resting over her breasts. She shivered. Mazvita was cold and afraid.

Her thoughts wandered everywhere. She remembered Nyenyedzi, but quickly thought of Joel. It was better to think of Joel than of Nyenyedzi. She thought again of Nyenyedzi. The memory frightened her. She pulled Joel's shirt from a suitcase filled with unwashed clothes, under the bed, and thought of Joel. Joel. She remembered Nyenyedzi.

Mazvita thought of Joel. The child belonged to Joel. At least that was a beginning. She replaced Nyenyedzi with Joel. She replaced Joel with Nyenyedzi. She thought of Joel. She grew faint and lay still once more on the bed. It shocked her that she was expecting birth, that she would be a mother. She had not been concerned with birth. She had simply not thought about it. "Nyenyedzi," she called.

She had no doubt of her calamity.

Joel, again.

∼

twenty

She found herself on the bus, not yet resolved on her destination, but ready to go somewhere. The bus stood still. Mazvita waited anxiously at the back, cramped in the last seat on the bus. The seat was covered with the cages and the boxes and the pillows and the plant seeds. This indiscriminate pile towered behind her. She shared her seat with two women who fanned themselves with flat knitted baskets. They were older women. They swung their heavy arms in wide arcs and frowned at the heat. Mazvita kept the baby tied to her back. The women looked at Mazvita curiously. They looked at the baby, whose head was covered with a white napkin. The napkin dropped from the mother's neck, where it was firmly tied.

Mazvita maintained a detached pose. She did not greet the

women. She held her face in an unwelcoming gaze. She raised her neck and kept it stiff and unreasonable. The pose was strenuous and surprising. She needed some kind of pose, she was sure. She needed new and untried gestures, and so she started with her neck, because that was where she felt most of her pain, that was where she felt she was living. The baby rested below her neck. She released the napkin and tied it up again, much more firmly. She could hardly breathe. It was not enough. She made another knot above the first.

She could not afford to be discovered.

She pulled her neck up, above the heads of the two women. She opened her eyes wide and tried hard to keep them open. She had to keep her world in focus, or else it would change shape. She sorrowed in profuse echoes of dismay and loneliness. It was like that for her. Mostly, she feared her world would move into another room in which the door was tightly shut against her. She had conceived of such a deceptive maneuver while waiting outside the bus. Then, she feared that her world might enter the bus and leave her out of it. She had the wretched feeling of following her world around, with her eyes. It was hard for her to establish disguises that would permit her to be unrecognizable to her world, so that she could follow it successfully. It meant becoming a stranger to herself, first of all. Her eyes, therefore, were vital to her survival.

She could not afford to be unwary, to pause. There was such tension below her temples, such a confusion of racing footsteps. She had had to run when she thought she saw all traces of her world vanish. She hated the sound of her own footsteps because they grew upon each other, and she heard the footsteps when she ran this morning, and then she ran again, away from them, into another chaotic pattering. There was so little space inside her, nowhere for the sound of her feet to vanish. She stood still whenever she could. She grew stiff.

So she held her neck up, or at least thought she did, though in truth, she sat curled in a miserable hump of fear, her shoulders crushed. Her head leaned toward the window and knocked on it repeatedly. Her head dipped down. Her head swung sideways. Her head hung toward her back, toward her child. Her right hand was held stiffly in front of her, the fingers curled sideways, as though she meant to throw something out through the window but the gesture had turned too heavy for her. She seemed waiting for assistance, but her fingers were empty, and so no one offered to help. Her fingers remained in that awkward frozen motion. Her eyes closed into mere slits through which she allowed the world to squeeze in, and she saw everything in a blur. Her faintness increased as the heat thickened in the bus, as her vision dissipated. She might have chosen that moment to die.

Then she heard an old man play the *mbira*.

The old man sat curled midway in the crowded bus, along the aisle. He was squeezed narrowly on the edge of the seat. He held the *mbira* possessively above his lap, and played. The *mbira* sat in one half of a dried shell, a calabash. This shelter made the sound fall backward, toward the back of the bus, where Mazvita waited. The gesture was unexpected and lavish. The sound reached her in generous waves of sustenance. Mazvita waited in a smooth and silent gaze. She turned her eyes from the window to the *mbira* and she cupped her fingers and held them forward. Her hands were still and seeking. The two women stared at her in amazement. Her eyebrows softened into arches of wonder. Her lips softened. The tightness disappeared along her neck. The skin on her neck grew smooth. The *mbira* was a revelation, a necessary respite. Mazvita waited with cupped hands.

The people in the bus continued their chatter, they laughed loud, told their children to sit still, coughed from the dust that fell in through the open windows . . . Mazvita listened through that din of voices and received the *mbira* sound, guided it toward herself. She held her fingers tightly together. It fell in drops, the sound, into her cupped hands. She found the *mbira*. It was beneficent. The sound came to her in subduing waves, in a growing pitch, in laps of clear water. Water. She felt the water slow and effortless and elegant. She breathed calmly, in the water. The *mbira* vibrated through the crowd, reached her with an intact rhythm, a profound tonality, a promise graceful and simple. She had awakened.

It was a moment too exquisite to bear and she folded her arms across her breast and closed her eyes tightly, for the joy was reckless and free, stirring and timeless. A lapse, and the *mbira* hid from her. She searched frantic and forlorn through the growing voices, searched and listened. She remembered the first notes of the sound she had heard. She found the *mbira* held in her fingers. She caught the *mbira* but it was elusive when it chose, thinned into slow sudden drops like melting heavy clay and she waited in a gasp so finely protected, waited in a calm and steady embrace of shadow and sound. The moment was precious. It hung on a delicate spot below her neck, at the back of her neck. The sound looped in waves over her head, curled downward, sunk deep into her chest where she had been irrevocably wounded, touching her gently and faithfully, tenderly and with mercy. There was forgiveness because she longed for it. There was forgiveness as she desired it, reconciliation and dream. She heard the *mbira* grow loud, move nearer to her, nearer to her dream. She waited in waves of suspenseful wishing and longing, in rays of supple joy. She sat still, waited though she knew deep down that her waiting was futile and misguided. The moment was intimate, irresistible and plentiful. She had longed so hard she had forgotten this was longing and yearning and desire. She remembered. The *mbira* was a splendid remembrance. She fought for a memory brilliant as a star, but there was darkness so deep and silent, and now, this glorious searching sound visited her, sought her out, found parts of her which were still whole, which held some sweetness and longing. The *mbira* grew loud

and heavy like a thick shadow. It grew loud to bursting and she retreated. She could not risk such climactic yet hopeless tributes. She
heard the sound encroach, poised and inviting. The *mbira* covered her
across her shoulders, crept into the hidden spaces between her fingers.

She felt a movement. She allowed herself to hope. Mercy. Mercy. She
waited for a moment merciful with release, for the *mbira* held out a
promise. She welcomed the *mbira* which brought to her a sky flaring
with waves of white cloud. The *mbira* led her across a white sun. She
waited for the sound to circle her with a new promise of freedom. Her
arms trembled because she feared waiting. Her eyes opened bright and
full of hope. She waited eagerly and trembling. Then the sound died. It
died in slow undecided rhythms, as though someone hit hard at the in-
strument with a fist. The notes collapsed.

She looked up.

∼

When the sun began licking Mazvita's face she could smell the paraffin in the room. She had not slept. She always noticed the paraffin stove as soon as there was enough light in the room. She woke to the reeking smell. The stove rested on a raised platform at a corner of the room, where it was held tightly on a small wooden box.

Yesterday she had opened and pushed new cords into the stove, pushed them forward. Her fingers smelled of paraffin. She hated the lingering smell, the burnt smell of the smoke as it filled the room, entered into the food, tarnished everything. Clothes were hung in another corner of the room, along a line of pegs against the wall. The clothes, like the walls, bore the paraffin smell.

They hung limp and dark with the paraffin. The house was small and ready to burst into flame. The blaze would begin from her fingers. They carried such a continuous stench. She imagined the flames lighting that limited room. The smell entered everything. Paraffin, life in Harare, life with Joel. She thought, she breathed, she slept. The paraffin was inescapable.

Running footsteps covered the tarred road, and Joel woke up. People were running to catch buses and travel the distance into the city. She could imagine them, shadows in the half-light carrying their food tins that were filled with last night's leftovers; a bit of meat, some sadza, and perhaps a piece of bread added hurriedly by a concerned wife. She was not a wife, not in that specific sense. There were not many wives, like that, in Harare. Lighter footsteps, and the soft chatter of women going to their jobs in the city. She could never tell Joel. She buried the child. She was submerged in her secrets, and she breathed hard, like drowning. She had died silently with the thoughts she kept to herself. She could not hold her breath, like this, for much longer. Joel.

Joel snored oppressively beside her, she thought he had woken up. Had she not heard him stir? She could not bear to wake him for work. She could not stand the sound of him, or the smell of him. It surprised her that they lay so close to each other's dreams, and did not know each other's secrets. Did Joel not see that her stomach had grown, that she ate less, that her face had fallen? Did he know nothing of what she suffered? He groaned, and she turned away from him. He groaned and turned, rolling over to her side of the bed, as though to push her off.

Mazvita held her hands against his sweaty back, creating a barrier across which he could not move. Even this action that protected her from falling off the bed pained her, and as he settled again into restful sleep, she let him go. She hated to think of the baby. She thought of the baby. She passed a searching hand over her stomach. Her stomach stiffened. She swallowed the harsh paraffin smell.

She balanced carefully on the edge of the bed, suspended in the memory of their first encounter.

≈

twenty - two

Joel ignored the baby. It was not his. He wanted the baby to disappear.

Mazvita had deceived him. Her deception was final and inexcusable. He had no doubt that she knew about the baby, hid the fact from him, because she was desperate. He forgot all about the innocence he celebrated in her. She was like any other woman. He saw her pretending to fall off the bicycle when they first met. She had been so clever. The baby arrived seven months after they had met. Joel did not believe that Mazvita had not known anything about the baby.

Mazvita was as surprised as he was, and felt disgraced by the way her body had betrayed her. She wished the baby belonged to Joel. The baby belonged to her alone. She did not understand how the baby had chosen her like that, creeping into her life, surprising her. She had woken up one morning with a strong sense of something irretrievable and wrong. She felt a bitterness on her tongue, in her throat. She ignored the feeling for days, though she grew dizzy and weak and could not swallow food. Always, when she got out of bed, her knees shook and failed to support her weight.

She told Joel about the baby and her misery.

In all the months she waited she closed the thought of the baby away. She simply waited. The waiting was separate from the baby. She waited only for the bitterness to leave her tongue. She hated that bitterness which made her tongue heavy, which made her unable to sleep. If Joel did not want the baby, she would also not think about it.

She wanted to stay with Joel. She had settled into the easy undemanding method of their life together. She had been looking for employment and felt an eagerness concerning what awaited her in the future. She was sure to find a place to work. She had meant to surprise Joel, to surprise herself with her success. Her freedom came in soothing waves of forgetting, in her increasing distance from Mubaira. She entered slowly into her life in the city, but with unmistaken resolutions.

Then the baby arrived, just like that. She had no name for the baby. A name could not be given to a child just like that. A name is for calling a child into the world, for acceptance, for grace. A name binds a mother to her child. A name is for waiting, for release, an embrace precious and permanent, a promise to growing life. She had no promises to offer this child. Mazvita could not even name the child from the emptiness which surrounded her. She simply held the child, and fed her from her breast. The child grew in a silence with no name. Mazvita could not name the silence.

It was futile, remaining with Joel like this. Mazvita understood that she had to leave. She stayed on. He became violent with his words. He chose his words well, for he wanted her to leave. She stayed. She needed more than words to initiate her departure. She knew she had to leave, would leave.

Then one morning, she woke up in a sweat.

~

twenty-three

1977. People were known to die amazing deaths. Natural deaths were rare, unless one simply died in sleep.

The people on the bus knew the truth about their own dying, but they had a capacity to evade uncomfortable realities. It was a risk to be on a journey, to travel. Traveling was a suspension of all pretense to freedom. Traveling made living real. The road was cluttered with dead bodies and held no promise of growth. A road was not for pursuing destinations: a road was another manifestation of death.

1977. It was a time for miracles. If you arrived at your destination still living, then you prayed desperately to continue to live. It was hard in those rural landscapes. There were all kinds of horizons witnessed, all kinds of sunsets. The sky was embroidered with new suns, for it burned even in the middle of the night. The sunsets were brilliant and unimaginable. A war has amazing sunsets.

1977. Everyone was an accomplice to war.

The war made them strangers to words. They shaped any truth which comforted them. The war changed everything, even the idea of their own humanity. They were shocked at what they witnessed and lived through, what they were capable of enduring, the sights they witnessed. They welcomed silence. If they spoke with energy and abandon, it was to fill the empty spaces left by those who had died marvelous deaths, who had vanished in the midst of their journeying. The war made the people willing accomplices to distortions—distortions solitary and consoling.

People lived with their feet off the ground, though they indeed traveled. There are stranger truths in the world. The war made the people generous with their bodies. They offered their bodies for their improbable journeying. They were welcomed, and feasts prepared for them, even before they entered the road. It was known they were coming, and those who knew about their coming welcomed them, days before they arrived. It was not known what would happen to the body as it journeyed. A journey was not to be trusted. Only the promise to arrive could be resurrected and protected.

The travelers were not surprised when the bus sank downward, as though a new weight had been added to the roof. The bus stopped in the middle of the road. The stopping was abrupt, threw them forward, and they fell back into their seats.

They searched the opaque windows, and saw through the dust the lines of police vehicles. The faces were brown and buried, indistinct, minute. The heads were missing from the shoulders, the arms chopped off. The windows were thick with dust. The people searched fearfully behind the sheltering glass in a temporary refuge for their fear.

A policeman went round to the driver and spoke to him. The driver moved from his seat and descended the stairs to the door. He pushed hard at the door with his shoulder. The door flew open. Metal banged on metal. The driver leapt out of the bus, so did the conductor. The people sank further into their seats.

Mazvita. She watched a soldier standing under the dusty window. He held a gun close to his body, close to his face. His face was scarred. She stared at the scars on the face of the soldier. She wanted to stay on the bus when she saw everyone move down the passage, lifting their heavy boxes and their wares. The face she thought she had recognized moved toward her and knocked hard with the gun against the window, so she moved forward, like everyone else. She had hoped the soldier would know her.

"Bring all your bags," a voice bellowed into the bus.

The conductor leapt to the roof of the bus and untied the goods. The untying was laborious because the goods had been tied in firm knots for the long journey, to resist the uneven road. A soldier barked at the conductor. He worked at the ropes, in that heat, in that fear, in that promiseless sky. He searched his pocket rapidly, found a knife, and sliced through the knots. The suddenness of release sent some of the goods falling on one side of the bus, and the driver ran forward. A table tumbled and crushed on the side of the road, sideways, its legs curved inward.

The soldiers rummaged furiously through the goods, tossed garments in every direction, whispered endless prophecies, asked the women to stand on one side of the road, with the children. Mazvita. Her eyes were clear of tears.

～

twenty-four

Mazvita dreamt the child had vanished. She screamed till Joel woke her. He insisted, even in the middle of the night, in the midst of her violent dream, that she must leave on that morning.

"Leave me," he said. He swung his body away from her. She heard his knees hit against the wall. He pulled his legs back, and slept. He slept while she turned and tossed.

She offered to take the baby away to her home, and then come back to him. "That is good," he said. He was so quick with his answer she knew there was no hope of finding him waiting. Instead, she conceived a deep hatred for this man who found it impossible to accept her and the child. He denied her an opportunity she had sought, to grow. She did not ask for love from him, just acceptance. Instead, Joel interrupted her every thought. He had wearied of her presence.

It was as though she was living with two men. When she thought of Nyenyedzi, she loved the child deeply. She called the child Nyenyedzi, in her dream, because the child was a boy. When she thought of Joel, she wanted the child to go away. She had no memory of being close to this child, even while it grew inside of her. She had no memory of this child growing inside her. She fed the child from her breast, and turned her eyes away. Her breasts felt heavy with the milk for this child. The child had brought its own milk. It had definite plans about its own survival. Joel stayed from her milk and her child. Mazvita grew thin with her thought. She had such dreams.

She dreamt of Nyenyedzi. She dreamt of his tenderness and promises. She wished that she had stayed with him as he had asked. She wished she had known about the child before she left. She would not have left. She longed for Nyenyedzi. She dreamt that she met him and showed him the child. He rejected the child saying it was not his. He would not accept her. It did not matter to him how much she had suffered to bring his child into the world. Nyenyedzi stayed away from her milk. Mazvita had no memory of giving birth to this child. Joel told her it was her child. Mazvita held the baby close to her breast.

One morning, after she had again woken dripping in a sweat, Mazvita sat by the window and watched the child as it lay on the bed, in that room small and dark. The walls were dark, the curtains hung in shreds of dim light. She heard the soft whir of the paraffin stove, because she had lit it to boil some water. She heard the flame blow against the surface of the kettle. The room, the curtains, the bed. She held her nose in distaste. Mazvita disliked the paraffin smoke, which she had to rub off the pots.

The lower part of her right palm was black with oily smoke.

~

t w e n t y - f i v e

The City.

Clothes hung on wooden figures, on women still, thin, and unmoving. The figures offered no names, no memory. The past had vanished. Perhaps they offered beginnings, from the outside in. One could begin with a flattering garment, work inward to the soul. It was better to begin in sections, not with everything completed and whole. It led to such disasters, such unreasoned ambition. So the dresses hung limp on the women, offering tangible illusions, clothed realities. These glassed and protected women had long brown hair and red lips and arms stretched, offering a purchasable kind of salvation. The figures had a rare insight into bodies, with no breasts, yet their children stood with them in equal poses of divinity. The children held plastic arms toward their mothers. The children wore lace. They wore bright red ribbons. It was difficult to understand the exchange the children offered because it was so clear that they had not begun to live, that their parents, standing holier above them, had at least some form of pretense—long smooth necks held out to the day, heads bent slightly inward, as though they served tea. It was like that with the figures, an austere reality, fixed, with handbags held across arms stiff and long. Silent eyes fixed on passersby. The eyes saw and spoke nothing. The eyes were voiceless. They burrowed, ate their own bodies.

The ritual was cruelly imitated.

∼

t w e n t y - s i x

"When are you leaving?" His tone was abrupt. She dared not answer him. Instead, she fed the baby. He looked quickly round the room. His eyes darted over the head of the baby, darted across her breasts, across the window into the dark. He skirted, swung onto the bed, and took up a book. He flipped through pages.

Mazvita fed the baby slowly and patiently. She observed Joel's every quick move. She saw a finger pass over his tongue, then pages flip, read backward. He snapped his fingers, accompanying some tune held in his head, placed the book under his shoulder where he rested on the bed, closed his eyes, snapped his fingers in a fast rhythm she could not follow. He closed her out. Whistled. He snapped and whistled.

Joel jumped up from the bed and opened the window. The

window creaked. The window creaked, and closed. The pages rustled.

Mazvita fed the baby slowly and patiently.

The bed creaked. The question leapt at her. Mazvita turned her face slowly toward him. She sat on a mat on the floor. He looked, looked away, looked again. Feet swung from the bed to the ground. Her heart beat fast because she thought he had made an irrevocable decision that excluded her immediately. She moved the baby from her breast.

"When are you leaving?"

Joel moved back to the small window and lifted the curtain. A dog howled in the distance. Joel let the curtain fall. He stood with his back resting against the wall. He took several quick steps around her, cast a brisk but penetrating stare at the baby. He vanished behind her.

She gasped. His voice was swift.

"Leave. Tomorrow," he said with a prompt emphasis.

Her decision came to her slowly. When it did come, she was not sure that the decision had been entirely her own.

~

twenty-seven

She had stopped thinking of Nyenyedzi and Joel. She thought of Joel. She remembered the morning, running. She no longer thought of that man while she was awake. She kept trying to find his face and all she felt were his arms over her legs, pulling her down. She was sure that if she remembered his face, she could free herself of remembering him. She could replace his face with another, with beginnings. She searched for his face. She felt arms circling her legs, coiling over her, and she fell onto the stranger. She fell on his outstretched legs. It was as though she had tripped and fallen down, except she had felt the pull on her legs. He pulled at her. She did not cry but struggled slowly against him. He whispered in harsh lulling tones, whispered persuasively, demandingly, and pulled her roughly toward him. He whispered that he did not have time to talk to her. He whispered about the things he did not have time to do. "Maybe you have time for all these things," he informed her. He spoke with his face turned from her. She thought only of being buried, of dying slowly after he had killed her. She believed she had died except she felt his hands moving over her shoulders. He was determined to discover parts of her that were hidden to herself.

The morning covered her eyes, her feet. He parted her feet and rested above her. His face was turned away from her. He kept his face hidden, and whispered repeatedly to her. He tore at her dress, pulled her legs away from her. He removed her legs from her body, and she lay still, not recognizing her legs as her own. The mist hung on her forehead, behind the armed man, only his hands rested on her shoulders and kept her pinned on the ground. He slid above her, beneath the shelter of the mist.

Then she ran. She heard him behind her when she started to run into the morning. She ran but the morning was full of his whispers, of his arms moving beneath her body, of his hidden face, of his fingers pulling at her feet, of his stale and damp clothing. She ran from him, ran from the things he had whispered between her legs.

She ran from the rising mist, from the morning.

She forgot about Nyenyedzi and Joel. She remembered the mist and the whispers.

∿

t w e n t y - e i g h t

This hole is so deep and so old and heavy on my back. Joel, this body is not me sinking into this hole so deep and dark. Where can I go and remain whole? Who will help me carry this pain? Where will I speak this tale, with which mouth, for I have no mouth left, no fingers left, no tears to drink. Let me thirst and die. Let me lie down and die because I have died in this sleep. What is it that came to visit that left foot marks here and there and every- where? It left its skin right there on my path for me to nest under. I will be buried in a skin unknown and strange. Joel, I hear a fly buzzing all around. It is buzzing around the head of my child. Is that the hole dug for me, so deep, and that fly buzzing over my head sent from that hole? Who will hear my song? Who will carry it for me this pain and this suffering heavy on my back? I have turned and turned in my sleep dreamt of mountains such mountains growing on my back. Let me walk onto that mountain growing on my back . . .

She had not anticipated such a hollow feeling, such emptiness. The child brought to her such powerlessness she could hardly move forward. Mazvita could not remain where she was because Joel forbade it. He suggested that she move backward, into the past. Her instinct was to dream new dreams. There was such a heaviness in her arms. Mazvita longed to release the heaviness that made her unable to spread her arms and embrace the future. She wanted her arms but they were heavy with the child. Mazvita sought the path that led her here. She gathered her footprints till they disappeared from her vision. The past was more inventive than she was, laid more claim on what belonged to it. The baby had chosen her, risen above its own frailty in order to hinder her.

Mazvita felt betrayed.

~

twenty-nine

The bus plunged into clouds of thickening red dust. Mazvita was surprised to hear laughter on the bus. It was as though the laughing had moved from inside her into the bus, into the mouths of strangers. She had preferred the laughter when it was silent, and completely hers. Now she had to laugh together with the strangers. She heard the two women in the seat ahead.

Mazvita had to laugh with the women too. It was not clear why they laughed, but one of the women pointed to a cloud of heavy dust coming through the window and leaned forward to fight against it. But the window had tightened and the woman had to fight hard to close the window. When she finally pulled back her face was covered with the dust. Her face was red. The people laughed. The people in the bus laughed about the dust covering the woman. Their laughter must be different from hers, then. Mazvita did not share the safety and certainty held in their laughter, so she felt assured that they had not stolen her secret. Mazvita felt rescued. She searched through the dust covering the window, through the clouds growing outside as the bus journeyed forward. She would arrive soon.

She turned her eyes back to the bus and found the women still laughing. Mazvita knew enough about her own survival to know that she had to laugh with the others, to throw her arms and meet those of the other women halfway across the seat, to glance at the men and see how they laughed at the woman. To laugh with the men. It was a chance to dispel suspicions regarding her apparent silence. It was difficult for her. She leaned forward and protected a pain beneath her chest. She could not laugh with the women, loud like that, when the pain threatened repeatedly. She closed her eyes.

Mazvita closed her eyes and saw the dust all over the woman's face. The woman had returned from the window to her seat. The woman followed Mazvita into her dream, into the place she chose to hide. Mazvita could not keep the woman from following her. She remembered the soldier she had seen through the window. The soldier must have shot this woman, because he had stood on just this side of the road. No. The woman was still living. It was only that she, Mazvita, had closed her eyes to keep the woman away. There had been no soldier on the side of the road yet Mazvita remembered that the soldier had held a gun. Where had she met the soldier, then? Mazvita felt a dizzying and painful motion stir inside her, with her memory. She folded her chest and felt the baby shift on her back. It was important to keep the strange woman away from her. The woman remained far away, beyond Mazvita's closed eyes. She must not think of the woman. The woman had been killed by the soldier. The soldier had killed her, after . . . Mazvita could not remember the event after which the woman had met her death. Certainly, death had come slowly to the woman. Mazvita told herself to remain calm, though her heart beat rapidly. It would not be long before she, Mazvita, left this bus. She was safe. She must keep the dead woman away from her thoughts. Dust fell over the woman's hair, which turned red like the clouds outside.

Mazvita had not spoken throughout the trip. Now she moved her lips slowly and painfully, though no one listened to her, not even the woman who followed her into her thought. Mazvita spoke about waiting for the bus. The waiting had not been for long. Mazvita spoke about the tie she had left on the bed. Joel must not miss his tie. She could not remember if she had left the tie on the bed or on the table. She could not remember clearly and felt her heart beat beneath her chest. Perhaps she had brought the tie with her. Where was the tie if she had brought it with her? She should have talked to the woman who sold her the white apron. She was sure the woman would have listened. She saw the woman smile and hand her the folded apron. The woman folded the apron slowly and carefully, as though she acknowledged the long distance Mazvita had to travel before unfolding it again. Mazvita received the apron and held it in one hand. She pulled the hand over her chest. She did not wait long to unfold the apron. She saw her child within every fold of that apron, as it fell open toward the ground. Mazvita moved her lips slowly as she remembered the apron unfolding. She heard the women laugh in the background and thought it was only her own voice murmuring into her memory, murmuring softly and mutely.

Then Mazvita saw again the strange woman carrying the dust on her face. Mazvita did not understand how the woman had continued to follow her through the things she said to herself, that she expressed in her quiet gestures. Yet she had felt the woman constantly there, seeking to find her. The woman sought to discover the things Mazvita left un-

said. Mazvita saw the woman lean toward her and tell her to remove the
child from her back. Mazvita heard the awful cry leave her, heard the bus
turn to silence. Mazvita had not wanted to awaken like that. Again she
cried pitifully. The woman told her to release the child from her back
and allow the child to play. Why did she not allow the child to play? She
was a cruel woman to her child, keeping her on her back all the way on
the bus. A child must not be kept on the back for such a long time, and
in this heat. Did she not know that this heat could kill her child? She
must remove that napkin from the baby's head at least. Mazvita spoke,
the woman spoke. Their voices were one. The woman spoke with
Mazvita's voice. Mazvita had not heard her voice for a long time and it
shocked her to hear her own voice come to her from the woman, so
clearly pronounced. Mazvita laughed. She laughed with the voice of the
woman, which was also her own voice. Mazvita cried to the woman to
keep quiet but the woman leaned over the seat and repeated the same
words, in the same voice that belonged to Mazvita.

As the woman spoke, as Mazvita spoke, Mazvita felt an awful piercing beneath her breasts. Her lips shivered with the cry that spread outward from her chest. It spread beneath her eyelids. Mazvita knew that
the woman had stolen her thought and that there was no use fighting
her. Mazvita answered that she would release the baby very soon.
Mazvita answered with two voices, both of which were hers. Then she
felt the woman bend forward and start to untie her apron. She was a
daring woman indeed. She had such fire in her eyes, such a determined
frown. Mazvita allowed the woman to untie the apron. She could not
stand against such a determination. After all, the determination was her
own. She wondered why she would do such a foolish thing as allowing a
strange woman to expose her, to uncover her secrets, to speak with her
own voice, but she felt tired of fighting. She longed for a comforting

anonymous face. She longed to be discovered, to be punished, to be
thrown out of the bus. It was better for her than to continue on this
journey. The dust spread evenly over the window, in thick red clouds.
She could not survive the journey. Mazvita felt the woman touch her beneath the chest. The arms belonged to Mazvita. Mazvita moved her own
arms toward her chest. She rested the fingers over the knots and allowed
the woman to proceed. She would not help the woman to uncover her.
Mazvita's body rose up, against the woman. Mazvita had tied the apron
tightly beneath her stomach. Again, she felt a tremor over her arms, and
she cried weakly. The untying was difficult for the woman and she
cursed as she struggled with the thick cloth. Mazvita was determined
not to help the woman and held her fingers tightly over the knots.
Mazvita closed her eyes again and felt the stranger free the child. The
child fell from her back onto the seat and this woman with dust on her
face this woman she thought was herself told her to hold on to the child.
Mazvita took the child and held the child in her arms. The child's head
had grown soft. The neck had grown wide. The child had been growing
on her back. She did not recognize the face of her child. Mazvita tried to
hide the neck of her child. She told the strange woman that her child
was sick. She must keep her child on her back where it was quiet and
safe. The woman seized the child from her and brought it to her own
breast. She would feed the child because it was hungry. Why had she not
fed the child in all their traveling? What kind of child slept so soundly
when there was such a noise on the bus? Then the cry exploded in her
again and Mazvita opened her eyes and found her fingers clasping the
tied ends of the apron. The apron was still tied to her back. The knot
held firmly above her breast. Mazvita reached cautiously and felt the
baby still fastened on her back.

   Mazvita turned to see that the woman was wiping her face with her scarf, and the wiping made the men laugh even more because it left the woman's head bare, and her hair was gray. The men laughed at the woman because her hair was gray. The women laughed with the men. Mazvita laughed with the women and the men. Her laughter was secret and whole.

Mazvita rubbed the dust, slowly, from her own eyebrows.

~

t h i r t y

Mazvita sat on the edge of the narrow bed, and held her hands tightly together. The baby lay in the middle of the bed.

Mazvita took the baby and rested a cold palm over its eyes.

She wanted the baby to close its eyes. Mazvita wept silently, because she knew that her desire for the baby to sleep was ill-conceived and harmful. Her heart beat so hard at her effort to suppress that inclination, but the desire lunged forward like something sweet and secret. She thought of sleep. She thought of loneliness and sleep. The feeling was overwhelming. She trembled beneath that thought. She closed her eyes and felt a cloud rest over her shoulders. Her shoulders felt heavy. She opened her eyes and thought of the child. She wanted to forget the child and creep back into that billow above her shoulders, crawl into a lethargic sleep.

She looked at the baby resting with its eyes opened. If the baby had fallen asleep right then she would have recovered from the madness that made her press her palm down, again, over the baby's eyes. Mazvita was still aware of her danger. The baby should have slept of its own accord right then, but it did not. She pressed her right palm softly, once more, over the baby. She felt the child's warm eyes under her palm.

That pressing granted her an elaborate and fierce energy to free herself from this baby, it drove her into a violent but calculated trance as she moved forward toward the child and picked it up from the bed, picked it up slowly and finally, picked it up in sobs that rendered her body into half, in sobs. She picked up the baby slowly, as though not to waken it. Her desire was to close the baby's eyes finally and truthfully. Mazvita sought her freedom in slender and fragile movements, finely executed.

Mazvita sang slow and dear to the baby that she felt was hers, was not hers, was hers, was not hers. She paused as though to comfort the child, touched it with one smooth gaze, as though to protect it. The child had deep bottomless eyes. She longed to close the eyes of her child, slowly and gently. The thought brought her an easy satisfaction, an exultant realization of a pleasure ephemeral but true. Joy beckoned in lilting waves of mercy and comfort.

Mazvita took a soft thin cloth and wrapped it over the child's eyes. The cloth smelled of milk. She had used the cloth to wipe the curdled milk from the side of the baby's mouth. The cloth fitted across the child's head, and she was able to tie it at the back. She made the knot very softly, whispering to the child to keep still. She made a soft painless knot that kept the child free from harm. The child listened to her slow cautioning movements, and kept still. This was a beginning. When she had completed this task she felt more sure of the direction in which she would proceed, she felt herself gifted and supreme, autonomous in all

her decisions, in her every gesture and action, and she breathed hard
and inward and felt the air flow into her chest. She had closed the eyes of
her child. Her breath returned to her in short repeated spurts.

She leaned forward and held the child's face in a lengthy and purposeful scrutiny. Mazvita moved forward once more, toward the child.
Water broke from her forehead and fell over the child's eyes, which were
hidden. It fell in dots over the milk cloth. The cloth was damp with the
water from her forehead. Mazvita noticed the dampness and felt an intense loneliness meet her in that silent room. She got up in slow measured steps from the bed, leaving the child.

She returned to the bed and sat down. Her arms reached toward the
child.

She was alone. She felt threatened somehow but did not understand
all the permutations of her misery. Only that her arms waited, and that
the dampness across the child's eyes had come from her. The baby
belonged to her, and she was alone. She whispered softly, about her
loneliness.

Her arms waited for the child.

She sat with the baby held in a blindfold across her arms. Mazvita
searched the room with her eyes. She did not quite remember being in
this room before, though it was familiar. She searched, aware that the
moment was vital and she could not let it pass without something
gained toward her release, not when the moment had come to her like
this, like sleep. The baby relaxed in Mazvita's tight grip, perhaps it had finally closed its eyes. But Mazvita missed the baby's signs of cooperation
because she had already wandered far and distant. She had discovered
and reached a completely new horizon.

Her determination was amazing. She stood outside her desire, outside herself. She stood with her head turned away from this ceremony of
her freedom, from this ritual of separation. She saw nothing of the wild-

ness in her actions, of the eyes dilating, of her furrowed brow, of her constricted face, of her elongated arms, of her shoulders stiff. She mistook her resolve for kindness. She saw nothing of her tears, yet she cried desperately in that triumph of her imagination, in that rejection of the things that were hers, that were of her body. Her forehead broke into ripples. Water fell from her forehead to her eyes, and blinded her.

Her rejection was sudden and fierce and total. She stood with the baby balanced on one arm. She took a black tie from a rack in a corner of the room and dropped it over the child's neck. It rested over the child in a huge loop, which, on another occasion, would have made her laugh. She did not pause. She claimed her dream and her freedom. She was winged and passionate. She drew the bottom end of the tie across the baby's neck. She pulled at the cloth while the baby remained blinded and trusting. She strained hard and confidently though this pulling choked her and blinded her and broke her back. It was bold, this pulling of the cloth, and she held on till there was no cloth to pull because the cloth had formed one tight circle, the smallest circle there was, and so there was no longer any use to her boldness. No use to her boldness because her boldness had brought a terrible silence into the room. There was absolutely no movement, no movement even from her own arms. She noticed first the stillness in her arms. She noticed her arms.

Bewildered and standing outside her own self she remembered some of her action toward this child. She had managed a constricting knot from which the child could not survive. She felt the neck break and fall over her wrist. She felt the bone at the bottom of that neck tell her that the child had died. The bone broke softly. The sound of it lingered long after she had heard it. The neck was broken. Still, she held the knot firmly between her fingers, for a while longer. She released the knot. The head swung back and fell onto her palm, because she had broken it. She had broken the neck of her child.

The head fell forward and she saw the top of the child's head. She saw the soft part of her child where she had been waiting for the hair to grow. She passed a cold hand over that soft dying part, and felt the softness still there. It had sunk inward, that soft part. It was bare and unprotected. The hair had not grown on it. It was bare that soft part of her child where the hair had not yet grown. Soft, and dying. She held the softness gently on her palm. The neck was broken. Her look as she held the face of the child was lulling and tranquil. She longed, tenderly, for the child's hair that she had not seen.

She kept the cloth over the child's eyes and placed the child back on the bed, where she had begun. She sought to discover the path she had taken toward this particular horror, but the memory hid from her. It came in flashes of a fathomless and heavy guilt. Her fingers felt cold and separate from her. She sat in painful isolation, convinced that what had happened was not true at all, yet what was that blindfold on the child, when had she put it there? The unusual detail confirmed the horror in her head. A mountain grew in her head.

She was responsible for some horrible and irreversible truth concerning her actions. She held her breath tight, within her chest. There was a burning on her tongue. Her tongue seemed to grow in her mouth, into something large and unrecognizable. She could no longer breathe cleanly and regularly. The bitterness spread to her face, into her eyes. She closed her eyes and tried hard to collect her thoughts concerning the child. She did not want to think of the child. She thought of the child.

She sat still, and wondered. She stood up. Her feet felt heavy but she took a step forward, dragged herself back toward the child. Her elbows ached tremendously. She fell forward, near where the baby lay. She slumped onto the bed, reared her neck forward, and raised her arms. The action was unbearable. She untied the cloth from the child's eyes. The eyes were closed peacefully in sleep. She felt almost joyous because she recalled a moment when this was the simple fact she sought. She recalled such a moment. The child had closed its eyes willingly. The closing of the eyes was good, but she saw the neck collapse downward on the baby's chest. The neck was broken.

Perhaps the child was not dead. She carried the baby on her back. The child liked to be carried on the back. The child remained silent while Mazvita moved in quiet footsteps across the room. Mazvita moved back and forth, near the bed. She sang softly, her lips pursed slightly. She sang in mute tones, in muffled and confused cries, pleading, hoping the child would stir. She felt the small head slide down toward her left shoulder and the move was silent and familiar. The child had fallen asleep. She had to hold the child up because it had fallen asleep in that awkward position, so she bent her back and leaned forward and rearranged the baby and supported it with her cloth. She held the child's head up along her back with the cloth and went around the room because she wanted the child to sleep.

She sang a faint lullaby to which there were no words. She sang of dying mushrooms, the ones she had found.

Then she bent again and released the cloth. The baby slumped downward, curled into her back. She felt the child's silent fingers beneath her arms.

She had accomplished a tremulous vision. She was capable of brave pronouncements still. She would bury her child in Mubaira, then she would die. She would go to Nyenyedzi and give him his child. It was his child. She left the tie on the bed, for Joel. The tie belonged to Joel. He must not miss it. She found the bus station where she had arrived only a few months ago.

It fell in lumps, the milk. It fell from the baby's mouth.

≈

thirty-one

The bus continued to move.

Every sound seemed to listen for her, though she was the one who listened in a rare painful listening that crept across her back, kept still so painfully still the stillness made her sob a heavy sob that broke over her shoulders, trembled down to her feet, and she felt her toes turn cold, turn cold and still. She entered a bottomless ache that left her perspiring and gasping for one slice of moon, to heal her not regretfully, but with a brimming ululating sympathy. Bottomless, that ache, cold and still.

It was the stillness on her back, cloying and persistent, which bothered her, choked her, sent a small painful echo tearing across her breast, turned her lips a bursting black clay, clinging and cold. She felt her eyes sink into the darkness gathered somewhere beneath her forehead, beneath the eyebrows, a still cold darkness in which she was sure there was no recovery.

Her back was moist and heavy. The stillness called to her, soft, cold. She felt her toes tighten and grow stiff, felt her nails break and break tearing over her skin, felt her ankles burn an intense deep burning, licked with a flame she could not fathom, and she looked straight ahead, tried to hide from the sounds that surrounded her with a gay indifference, telling stories, free, unlike her who carried such a weight on her back.

She listened to every sound in her thought, and wept deep and slow for the stillness on her back, a heavy cold stillness that hugged her, spread its arms around her, with small cold fingers, so cold and small. It rested over her spine, this coldness. It tried to deceive her, for her back broke into sparkles of flame. A red spot of flame grew on her back, like life. She knew beyond that searing wave, she knew the beyond of it, the cold that was heavier than the heat, for the heat was light. It was light not like petals or sunshine or reveries. It was light like burning skin. It was heavy.

The bus was crowded. She heard everything in that crowded bus, but something larger than her listened to her, heard her, scorned her suffering. The something was mocking and spirited, she dared not find it out, it was something haunting and triumphant, enormous and penetrating. It was not possible that she had just suffered like that, without an audience. She deserved at least one ear into her secret.

Mazvita thought she heard a soft humble breath caress her back, a shifting spreading wetness like tears, warm and asking, then she panicked knowing that this was not life, but death.

~

thirty-two

It is yesterday.

The trees are heavy with pod. There are no leaves on the trees, only twisting long pods. The leaves have fallen down. Trees sound with the wind beating against the branches, knocking the pods together. A dry sound, then stillness rattling, loud, between the hanging pods and the empty branches. Mazvita looks up. The pods are long and oval in the bare branches, large and full of clustered seed. Leaves fall in the arid air, race into the grasses in a promise of growth. She looks up and sees a purple flower tucked beneath the dry hanging branches, nestling into another season of flowering. The flower rests in a bare tortured tree, surviving, resisting the wind and shaking pods. Trees flatten and spread against the sky, their skin falling and folding to the ground. The trees grow across the sky. Mazvita walks through a narrow footpath held between the hills. Before, she must have looked up like this, just like this, learning to forget, bare and troubled.

If she had no fears, she could begin here, without a name. It is cumbersome to have a name. It is an anchor. It brings figures to her memory. It recalls this place to her, which, earlier, she has chosen to forget. Names inspire an entire childhood, faces reaching and touching. She wishes to forget the names that call her own name, then the hills would name her afresh. She would have liked to begin without a name, soundlessly and without pain. She is frightened. She has begun poorly, with too many visitations. She sees her mother, old, coming toward her, calling, "Mazvita!"

Mazvita looks up and sees the rocks small and many from deep in the valley deep gray, with stones spread between mounds of earth and bare trees. The stones are spread in the sky, for the sky swallows everything, pulls one up, pulls the eyes. The hills are high and the sky grows from the mountains. The mountains push at her, push her from the path, against the burnt grass. New grass grows over the burnt grass. The rocks tumble down the mountain. It is not peaceful, but the sky makes the rocks seem harmless—mist grows over the hills and covers the rocks. Mazvita finds the path again. The mist fills her eyes and hides the sky. The mist is the sky. The mist is blue like the sky but she knows it is not the sky, it is the mist. The mist is the sky and the rocks on the side of the hill. The sky tumbles and falls. The mist spreads and folds over the mountains, in layers, over the falling rocks. She walks in a blend of mist and rock, the sky falling over her shoulders, brimming from the mountains, over her head.

It is yesterday. Mazvita sees the smoke and hills. The huts are tucked in the hills, built among the rocks, with winding paths and thorny furrows between them. The huts are buried in the smoke. Mazvita moves slowly toward the huts, toward the smoke. The smoke tarnishes the horizon.

It is yesterday.

The village has disappeared. Mazvita can smell the burnt grass, though most of it has been washed away by the rain. The soil is black with the burnt grass. Mazvita gathers the burning grass. She will carry the burning grass with her. She will carry the voices that she remembers from this place, from the burning grass. She has not forgotten the voices. The broken huts are dark with the smoke and the mist falls gently over the empty walls. Mazvita moves toward the huts. The smoke is long departed, but Mazvita can see it over the huts which have been burnt. It is yesterday. Mazvita walks in gentle footsteps that lead her to the place of her beginning. Mazvita bends forward and releases the baby from her back, into her arms.

The silence is deep, hollow, and lonely.

≈

UNDER THE TONGUE

FOR LILIAN B. MBOYI

Courage,

friendship,

love, these three.

After that,

we are as burnt as ash,

and lighter still.

A tongue which no longer lives, no longer weeps. It is buried beneath rock.

My tongue is a river. I touch my tongue in search of the places of my growing. My tongue is heavy with sleep. I know a stone is buried in my mouth, carried under my tongue. My voice has forgotten me. Only Grandmother's voice remembers me. Her voice says that before I learned to forget there was a river in my mouth.

She cries about the many tongues which lie in the mouth, withered, without strength to speak the memory of their forgetting. Such tongues do not bleed. They have abandoned the things of life.

I listen. A murmur grows into my awakening, from Grandmother. She wipes her forehead with her hand and her voice embraces all my fear. She leans forward with arms held tightly over her shoulders. Then she brings her arms like a gift toward me, and she pulls a root which has grown deep inside her chest. Her eyes pull this root from inside her and I watch her lips tremble, her arms so silent, her voice departed, her elbows bare. She pulls this root from her mouth, from beneath her tongue. I know that this root begins inside me and that Grandmother will find where it begins. I know she placed it there before I was born, before my mother was born. She bends forward, once more, her arms folded, and she waits, shivering with release. I know that her waiting is also her giving.

Her voice says we can touch the sky even if it is so far away. We cannot fear our silence, our desire, our release. When our voices reach the sky with their crying, rain will fall and cover the earth. The sky will become a river, Grandmother says.

Rivers begin in the sky. Rivers begin with our tears. Grandmother's cry follows me everywhere. I touch my tongue. It is heavy like stone. I do not speak. I know nothing of rivers. Grandmother is a river. I am not Grandmother. My arms spread over her shoulders and I rest my face along her face. I listen to her voice roll over her back, tumbling, and I laugh. Grandmother is a river. The river is inside her body. The river is held in her mouth, held in her body.

Grandmother will be carried by the river which waits inside her, waits to be remembered. I know if I do not enter the river I will never find her again. I listen to her cry which carries all my sorrow of yesterday and I know that I have brought this river to her. I am inside Grandmother. I am Grandmother.

It is not true that rivers come from the sky, she says.

I do not fear the darkness. Grandmother protects me with her weeping, tells me of the many places, the many sorrows, the many wounds women endure. She tells me about herself, about my mother,

Runyararo. Muroyiwa was the name of my father. Grandmother tells me about night, about my father. Muroyiwa. My father. This darkness is heavy as stone. Grandmother will teach me many forgotten songs.

She sings a lament. Not for silence, not for death.

A voice scrambles, turns into night.

Zhizha.

Father whispers an embrace of lightning. I bite hard on my tongue, hold my breath deep in my chest. My voice is sinking down into my stomach. My voice is crumbling and falling apart and spreading through his fingers. My voice hides beneath rock. My voice burns beneath my chest. Lightning finds me, embraces the moon, finds me fallen from the sky. I hear father.

Zhizha.

Singing . . .

Zhizha do not cry water is sleep not death.

But my voice is lost. Astray. Salt spreads through my eyes. My eyes are dry like stone. My voice blinded. My voice wishing to escape. My voice pulled from its roots, dug from sleep. My voice falling. My voice empty and forgotten. My voice slips in a dying whirl that grows small and faint. My cry is stolen.

I hear crushing in my stomach. Water pulling at my dream, pulling at rock, pulling at my sleep. I awaken. An embrace, once more, of lightning, entering my sleep.

A burning grows deep beneath the sky. A shadow grows on my chest, struggles to depart. I die in my sleep. My voice is held by the lingering shadow. I cannot speak. I lie inside stone.

Then a soundless cry, still and quiet . . .

sh sh sh

Father speaks in an unremembered voice. He has swallowed sleep. I see father waiting in my sleep. I see father in the midst of my cry. I see father. Father . . .

Zhizha.

He calls in a whisper and cry. Father . . . His voice is full of the unknown things of my growing destroying sleep. His voice says death is also life. He calls my name in the midst of night. Father . . . His whisper is heavier than night, than dream, than silence. He carries death in his arms, banishes morning.

Father holds my breathing in his palm. His palm is wide and widening, grooved and wet. Then he lifts a heavy arm and touches the edge of the moon, in my sleep. I shout through fingers so strong, so hard, his fingers saying in their buried touch,

Zhizha . . . Zhizha.

A hidden visit.

I cry but my cry meets silence. My voice has lost the promises of day. I hear my voice fall like a torrent down into my stomach. My voice meets rock, meets water, grows silent and dead. Father calls in my sleep. My voice grows still, and waits in a trembling quiet. I turn my face away and run from the moon. I listen. The moon banishes sleep and dream.

A shadow grows from the moon. The shadow lifts me from the ground. I wait beneath a fervent sky. The shadow of the moon has turned bright with the serenity of death. The moon is wounded by the darkness.

I search for the moon which has left the sky. Memory has left the sky. It is night.

. . . Zhizha.

I see a scar grow farther and farther. I am certain this is the path through which I will be born. The scar widens, peels like bark. I wait.

Father . . .

I do not want to see father, ever.

Your father has died, Grandmother says.

I turn away, sleep falling through my eyelids. Grandmother places a warm hand over my forehead.

Father has drunk the forbidden water from the sea, swallowed the deep unknown things of my growing, swallowed night. I see father, his forehead bruised. I heard him fall yesterday crushing like rock. He turns to me in the salt dark of the sea, saying,

Zhizha these are the secrets of the sea.

He reaches a cold hand toward me but I stand in sunlight, calling for my mother. I wait and wait. I have forgotten the song of my growing. I long to hear the name of my mother. I long to defeat the silence. I listen beyond the pounding of my heart, the pleading voice of my grandmother.

Zhizha.

Father died in his sleep, in his dreaming. I reach a trembling hand across his forehead. He breathes hard, saying,

these are the secrets of the sea.

No, in my dreaming. My hands held tight, my fingers crushed, my bones broken dry like rock so broken. I see Grandmother, a harvest of weeds covering her arms. Grandmother, embracing my cry. Father drowned while he slept.

The sky gathers both earth and cloud. The sky meets the river moving beneath stone. The river rises. Father pulls me down into the river.

He pulls at my dream and I sink beneath the pounding which falls through my eyes.

It is night.

Roots grow out of my stomach out of my mouth out of me. My cry is silence. My cry searches the river, wavers between bending reeds, finds father waiting and near. He holds my hand. He pulls hard at my arm. He pulls the roots in my growing, the dream in my belonging. I cry in a voiceless tremble, my eyes parched with darkness.

I close my eyes and do not speak. My mouth is covered with blood.

I call for mother but Grandmother says . . . do not be afraid Grandmother is here. I close my eyes and find a lullaby in my sleep.

I find Grandmother.

In my sleep.

∿

It was during the war that Muroyiwa looked for butterflies in the mountains. He had traveled a long way to the mountains to find them. When he arrived there he wondered what happened to the butterflies during a war.

His birth haunted him while he permitted himself to live. Permission, willed and visible, this living, because often he had to pause and think about his mother, being born, about the calabash. When next he died, it would be because he had succumbed to the will of another.

His mother spoke of retrieving him from a calabash. Muroyiwa failed to make tangible the distinction between any two emotions, so he pretended the confusion did not matter. He did think about it briefly between one breath and the next, and that

was not time at all. When he thought deeply about it, he felt like
an insect thrown defenselessly against the earth, not camouflaged
against the task of being so constantly threatened with living.

An insect. How else could his mother have managed to retrieve
him, limbs, arms, head, and toes, from a calabash, if he had not been an
insect? The calabashes he had seen were small. He could not imagine being retrieved from any one of them. Now that he was a man he could
not comfortably think of being born in a calabash, but his mother said
this had happened, and another further miracle, he had died at birth
then awakened the following morning, so they named him Muroyiwa.
The lulling ease with which his mother said he had awakened made
death seem similar to sleep, simply a wave of calm, not the tumult of
agony which the war married with death.

Folded into a calabash, ready for the burial which would occur in
the early morning, but Muroyiwa rose too with the morning. Afterward
the women could not bury him. They were not joyous either; they preferred him not to live. This was clear throughout his early life. To absolve
everyone of any malice in wishing him death, Muroyiwa quickly as-
sumed that death was better than life, more to be wished for. It was this
which made living tolerable, the constancy of death. Life tantalized him
with its promises of an ultimate and reachable fulfillment. Someone had
to be blamed other than himself for that struggle out of the calabash. It
was appropriate to say that he had been bewitched.

Muroyiwa had gathered death from inside a calabash and reduced it
to a shade of sleep. Such a light thing, this death, sweet, pulsating with
the eternity of sleep. When he first understood the meaning of his name
Muroyiwa could no longer escape from life. This he considered during
the war when he allowed himself to be haunted by beauty and loving
and the symmetry of mats, then he forgot about the war, or at least he
fought its encroachment. The war made him see clearly the objects he

wanted to see. It was like seeing thunder when the sky is black with rain. Muroyiwa was not blind to lightning, its tantalizing beauties.

War was black like the sky; beauty purified war. Then a desperate passion engaged him and would not let him free. Muroyiwa carried a calabash inside him, where his heart should have been, and there were no cobwebs of death in it, only an untarnished desire for living. He discovered the anxiety of death linked with the waiting that accompanied war. It was the waiting he fought against more than the war itself. He conceived a strategy to fight against waiting. This came in the pursuit of a limitless charm, of living. When he thought further on this desire he saw that such charm would not be found simply anywhere, but would be embodied in a form, perhaps that of a woman.

Muroyiwa became anxious. This anxiety of death, unlike other visitations, he understood without remorse.

A lack of remorse is not happiness, it is freedom from the anxiety of living.

≈

three

My eyelids collapse, heavy with sleep.

I hear voices filled with tears. Darkness trembles with the memory of the moon. It is night.

Grandmother cries for our origins. We met in water, she cries. Our dreams are birth and death.

In the gathering darkness Grandmother's voice rises piercing into the night, is swallowed by the darkness, returns in one tremulous echo, rises again surging forward, tumbling in a cascade bright with moon seeking the forgotten, the departed, who wait to be remembered.

We wait for healing mysteries to visit us. The horizon ripens a golden brightness growing in a splendid growth so rare. It is morning. I hear Grandmother sing a song about the sorrows of the world, the grief of yesterday which follows her. She sings about find-ing a memory in her dreams, a memory that will be for healing not sor-row. She sings about one large moon so large it carries many moons in it, hangs low as though it will touch the earth. Grandmother will harvest the milk of the moon for mother, for me. We wait.

I have searched the sky, Grandmother sings. It sits on my forehead, this moon. Grandmother says it is sometimes good to forget, to bury the heavy things of now, the things which cannot be remembered without death becoming better than life. Such things are for forgetting, for bury-ing beneath the earth. But a woman must remember the moment of birth and of death.

I hear my cry carried in Grandmother's mouth. She has found me. I am Grandmother. Grandmother cries for me and for my mother. She buries all our sorrows in her crying. Her cry swallows everything, swal-lows our fears.

Grandmother says we choose words, not silence. We choose words to bury our grief. A woman cannot say the heaviness of her life, just like that, without madness. A woman must speak the beauties and the sor-rows of the heart, she must dream a celebration. A woman must not for-get, she must not bury her sorrow and her dreams. If a woman buries her sorrow, a dream will kill her children. A woman sings the wisdom of her heart, sings her waiting, greets the moment of birth, defeats death and silence. Tonderayi, Grandmother cries about the forgotten whose sorrow has been awakened.

We met in water, Grandmother cries into mother's growing silence.

Grandmother cries to the stars and the shadows and the mysteries of the earth. She says I am part of her, that she is birth and dawn, she is mother. It is warm, she says. It is very painful but warm, over your legs, like waves. Birth is like water turning gently into cloud. We cannot hide our tears when sorrow has visited us like this, she says, our tears are as old as the daughters and mothers and grandmothers of our ancient earth, dear as birth, like morning and dew. These tears, they are warm like the earth, do not forget. We cry for birth and long to see ourselves in water. We seek our peace from the beginning of our being, from the mouth of rivers, from mothers. A daughter is the birth of dream, a daughter is daylight on growing leaves. Daughters are our mothers, Grandmother says. She carries my pain in her mouth. I know Grandmother will heal me with her word, her word that is for remembering all that has visited her suffering, that has accompanied my growing. Tonderayi . . . again she laments with all the moments of our birth.

Grandmother calls to me and to mother, Mother-of-Zhizha, she calls to my mother. Birth is the remembering of journeying, it is not to be forgotten. We are women. We belong together in an ancient caress of the earth. We are full of giving like the parting of clouds, gently falling, carrying the promises of growth, of a season serene with maturation.

Zhizha, Grandmother pleads.

It is night and Grandmother turns into an unforgettable whisper of lament. She throws our voices to the moon. She gives us a song for healing, for a memory without sorrow. The song buries all our desperation and our loss. Her voice rises and the moon grows bright into our dreaming, moving and turning a trembling light, round and smooth with her weariless giving. She throws our voices to the sky and night falls around our faces, feathery over our outstretched arms. The moon grows wide into the sky with Grandmother's calling, growing wide. The moon covers the sky.

Grandmother throws our voices to the moon. There are no stars in the sky only our voices. The woman on the moon is bearing a load on her head. She has traveled through the sky. She has seen all the pain of the world.

Grandmother's voice vanishes into the darkness. We wait. Her voice turns to a whisper thin with our desires. We wait for the unpredictable wonders that will beautify our dreams. We wait for morning. In our waiting a memory awakens our voices. Grandmother weeps. Her tears are darkness and dream. I will follow the shadow of the moon, Grandmother says of her pain. She calls, holding our dream between her fingers, fingers that are tender roots of fond longing. We witness the creeping of dew, on grass, in her dreaming.

It is morning. We remember the moon which has swallowed our voices.

We long to forget the thunder of departing innocence.

The sound tells me she has died.

I wait for the sound to tell me again that Grandmother has died.

I wait, afraid to move my feet, to breathe, move my arms, but the sound vanishes and refuses to return. I know that the sound accompanies her secret and her living and it is not to be forgotten. I turn my head rapidly to my left. I look again for the slow sound. My eyes search on the floor, everywhere. I search for Grandmother. When I find her she is resting still where I wait. I stand near. I stand near to myself. I see my legs, my feet, near Grandmother. I lift my arms and allow the air, thick, tainted with burning wood to move through me.

I am sure the heavy things of the world have entered Grandmother and defeated her, made her fall. She is so still it makes me tremble hard and fearful because I can hear again the slow heavy sound. The sound is behind my head, somewhere near, behind my ears. I dare not turn. I tremble till my trembling is quiet. I hate the quiet. It tastes like warm salt, on my lips.

Something moves between me and Grandmother and falls a great fall reaching my feet and slides between my toes. I hear the drops over my feet. I do not move. I watch my toes dissolve. I watch my feet which are no longer my feet. They are large, not quite there, not part of me. It is the same with my arms which have discovered their own ability for silence. Only my shoulders say these are my arms.

I raise my head up from the ground and from my feet, very carefully, and find the roof which seems so far away. My eyes fill with patches of soot. I search the wall's deep black, clotted with smoke. A flat winnowing basket is suspended against the wall. A frayed rope, once white, dangles over the basket and swings softly upward when I look. Behind the basket is the gray tail of a lizard. The tail is large and points downward, almost dead, like the rope. I wish grandfather would come home before I am swallowed by the things which have grown between me and Grandmother. Grown and grown.

I hide somewhere behind my eyes. I remember. I hide deep inside my head. Her falling like this has something to do with me, with my mother. I have brought this death to Grandmother.

Grandmother opens her eyes and asks for my name. I am quiet wondering if she thinks I am my mother. Runyararo, I say. A woman always remembers her child, Grandmother has told me. I am not Grandmother's child. She has remembered her child, my mother, not me. Runyararo . . . I say very loud.

The name falls and follows Grandmother to the ground and lies still. Runyararo . . . I do not understand why the name has followed Grandmother like that, followed us. I look for the name on the ground but I cannot move my arms. I cannot find the name with my arms. I do not move. The name lies still on my lips, watered with tears.

Runyararo . . . I carry the name in my mouth once more. It falls again. Runyararo . . . I search the ground through my tears. Runyararo . . . I see Grandmother. Runyararo . . . She closes her eyes again and sleeps. Her sleep has taken her and hidden her far where I cannot find her. I am afraid. I stand very far from Grandmother. I stand outside Grandmother, outside myself. I see mother. My mother not me my mother. Runyararo . . . I must give the name to Grandmother not mother. Runyararo . . . This is her name of birth and I must return the name to her where she can find it. I give Grandmother the name bathed with loneliness and longing. Runyararo. This word will heal Grandmother.

I remember the darkness and the night which have visited. I have to remember because the darkness has something to do with Grandmother being on the ground like this. Something helpless. The darkness has no shape or sound, just falling and dying and never getting up, like Grandmother. I know the darkness is just inside my head, somehow, waiting. It is not even inside my head. The inside of my head is not blue like morning though when I remember a blue like that it presses hard on my forehead and makes me cry. The inside of my head is wide. I know this from the pounding on both sides of my head. The inside of my head has swallowed darkness. Perhaps it is the sky which has entered me because sometimes I can see the morning rolled inside my head.

Grandmother says the sky is only words. The sky is inside us. The sky is hard to store in a small place even if it is only a word. The sky is water. Words are water too. I do not drown in the sky. Drowning is death. Grandmother says those buried in the ground have also drowned. A soft drowning of words. How can we be buried when no words have been uttered? Only words can bury us, she says. How can death arrive when the mouth has not allowed it to arrive? Death has a name which we can carry in the mouth without dying. Only words can bury us not silence.

In the darkness I see just one red dot and I can store it anywhere inside my head, even under my eye. I watch it move inside my head till it disappears. It grows very small. When I look at a small red dot it grows and fills my head. The darkness is very large. I am frightened. I hear Grandmother falling, dying. Runyararo . . .

Grandmother asks for my name again and I know she wants my real name not the name of my mother. Not mother, just me. My name not that of my mother. Grandmother says a woman's name is the one she has given to her child. Mother's name is me. Runyararo is the name of my grandmother because she gave the name to my mother. Mother carries Grandmother's name for her. I am mother.

Zhizha, I say. That is also my mother. I am mother. She is Grandmother. Zhizha is the soft fall of rain after harvest, a peaceful rain which is not for growing things but for mercy. It is a solemn kind of rain, lonely, with no song to it, just rain on brown leaves. Zhizha.

Harvest is green like birth. If a crop is not harvested it turns brown and dies. Water will not give it life. Runyararo . . .

The name falls in drops on my tongue like rain in late harvest. I give Grandmother the word which I have wrapped in leaves which are almost dead. I fold the secret into the shaking palm of her hand where my life begins, and she guards it with her tongue.

I ask Grandmother why she has fallen like that and she says she has forgotten where she was going, where she is, the places of her wisdom. My arms are empty, she says. My arms do not remember what they were carrying. She opens her arms and looks slowly downward to the ground as though she will recover something fallen there, as though she will pick a dream from the ground and place it back in her arms, nestle it where it has fallen from, in the warm crevices of her arms.

Grandmother asks me to tell her about the emptiness in her arms but I do not know how to begin. She wants to know how her arms found this emptiness because this emptiness is too heavy for her to carry, much too heavy for her arms. It is the emptiness which found her. Her arms would never betray her like this, she says, finding an abandon so rare and shattering that her mouth refuses to name it. Grandmother searches deep into her arms. There is nothing in her arms but her eyes searching through that nothing which grows with her every searching, with her every pleading, nothing at all but her empty arms.

I want to tell Grandmother about the slow sound of her dying but the nothing in her arms defeats everything. Only the basket on the wall is waiting perhaps with words to be shelled and tossed, waiting with words to be chosen, cast aside, separated, dismissed. I look at the basket and know that the best words are those that are shared and embraced, those that give birth to other words more fruitful than themselves, stronger than themselves.

Grandmother. Her eyes have swallowed the emptiness that has filled her arms. Her eyes brim with the same abundant nothing which has filled her arms and made her fall, which has broken her knees and made her into a child. Grandmother says she walked into a void, an emptiness so surprising her shoulders were thoroughly unprepared for it.

I move my feet toward the tarnished wall and reach for the basket. The basket is far above my head but the rope is nearer, so I pull hard at the rope which holds the basket to the wall and the basket falls into my waiting arms. There is a basket in my arms. I carry the basket across the silent room. I notice that my feet are my feet and I have also found my arms. I give the basket to Grandmother. I place it safely under her embrace. She touches my arms with a hopeful caress.

She moves her right hand inside the basket to gather something she has recently discovered, something that she has lost while gathering words.

∾

four

If there were any butterflies in the mountains, Muroyiwa
would meet their delicate caress like a restored blindness. He was
curious to meet butterflies amid the sound of death, the wailing
voices of women, the distresses of children, the dry desperation.

VaGomba was blind. Muroyiwa had been born into his father's blindness and it received and contained him like a vessel. At
birth, he had moved from the calabash into the blindness and because of this for him the butterflies surrounding the mountains
would be pitched louder than the sound of death. He had received
many longings from his father's blindness. There was death in the
mountains.

VaGomba. One morning a root had sprung from the earth
and torn the sight from his eyes. He had been digging, preparing

the fields for planting. Nearby was a large harmless stump. His hoe hit a root which sprung from the earth and hit him across the forehead, twice, across his eyes, like an angry whip. The whip was like trembling lightning. Unforgettable, merciless, the white root flashed a solid sound, then a sudden tearing gurgle filled the earth like a river before VaGomba fell into a sightless world. VaGomba, his face lacerated, curled his arms and rested them vigilantly over his eyes as though to protect them from a searing sun, lay still till the ground beneath stopped beating, his arms filled with blood, his temples bursting. Past noon, the shadows long, tense, pulling fiercely into the trees. In these taut rhythms they left the fields.

Before they left, VaGomba's wife, Muroyiwa's mother, VaMirika, picked up the discarded hoe and covered both portions of the split root hastily, furtively covered the blood which lay in dots scattered over the proud whiteness which was thick and bulging, buried the glossy root which was soft and slippery and harmless to her memory.

VaMirika went to her husband and tried to heal him. With her memory she again buried the deceptive root and its stealthy promises, leveled the ground with her foot, as though she no longer wished to touch the earth. She welcomed the ground's anonymity, its ability to forget tragedy no matter how bright with the color of surprise.

She could not bury VaGomba's sorrow as easily, however, his shimmering anger which made the day's shadows the longest of that planting season, the heaviest, carrying all the heaviness of their shoulders. VaGomba gently refused her hand and found the path leading home, on his own. He groped with his bare feet till he found the path worn to thinness, with its welcoming thorns and the undulating morning laughters they had left in the early dew. The laughter had grown coarse, their voices brittle and dry like crushed seeds.

VaGomba never spoke of this incident except he said that something truly tight had risen from the earth and unbound him, separated him from himself. "From now on I will only see my shadow and the shadow of everything that surrounds us." He remembered the shapes of things held in the hand, of pain held once across the eyes, recalled especially the feeling of that death. VaGomba found the shape of the absence of light, light traveling through water, on motionless lakes and rivers, and there was a sound to that light, through winds and the sound of that, light in the smoke above huts, and there was a sound too to that. In his mind the voicelessness of a single feather falling through light, meeting light wrapped upon a single grain of sand, moving above a yellow shoot of maize which has become a breath of fertile tenderness released kindly from the earth. The shape of the absence of light.

∼

A knife moves sharply on rock. I hear a cry like falling water, then silence.

I call in the night . . . Mother . . . Mother.

A knife moves sharply, over rock.

Mother . . .

I turn in my sleep. I listen. There is silence. A sound comes toward me. Thud, on the ground, at my feet. I run far into the night but I fall hard on the ground. Roots cover the ground, growing in knots, tightening, beyond my dream, into the morning. My legs and arms are caught in the ground pulling me down into a lake deep and dark under the tree. I turn and turn but my feet are buried beneath the earth. I pull hard but the roots grow from my stomach and pull at my sleep. Water everywhere. Water and night.

I sink, beneath dream. Thud. I wake from sleep. Then I turn again, and sleep. Nothing. My arms reach into the dark and search the silence. Nothing. Nothing but the fear growing across my forehead and blinding me. Night. Nothing but the soft night filled with the sound of dying dream, with my fingers, with my cry searching blindly. Thud. The sound moves upward and swallows the night. It dies slowly, in drops. My voice crawls out of my mouth and hangs somewhere beside that dying sound. The sound is me and I rise up to meet the darkness but the night is too heavy for my forehead and my arms. Something is held safely in my fingers, within the roots so many. I raise my feet from the ground, lift, shift, twist my arms. I pull my legs from the ground.

Roots grow from my knee, from my scar. I fold my knee and cover it with my hand and bury the secrets of my growing. The roots grow from deep inside my leg, from my bones. My scar grows wide. I listen to roots breaking softly in my bones. I listen to the softness in the silence. I remember my scar.

I hear a knife, moving sharply, over rock. A memory bursts from the sky, explodes in sharp piercing rays, burning, like flame. I run, my mouth covered in silence. I hear again the knife in the dark. I see mother. Mother. A door closes. Hard. The knife moves sharply again, on rock. A door opens and closes.

I hide under my tongue. I hide deep in the dark inside of myself where no one has visited where it is warm like blood. Night waits for my cry but I can only think of my knee bending slowly, painfully, touching the something, the nothing rising above my head, rising from my arms. I know this nothing is something, someone. I hear the door close. I do not want to think about this nothing which my arms remember, which has spread itself inside me, this something which hides. I fold my hand over my knee grown ripe with new wounds.

I run deep into the water my legs thick and heavy. I run. I fall. I fall a great height. I fall and fall and my voice meets me in collapsing waves, of sleep. My head is heavy because I have swallowed the water. My head grows and grows into my eyes. I have swallowed the gentle voice of my grandmother which pulls me from the river and I sleep a quiet sleep.

Grandmother is singing in the river. She sings about rivers which fold into the evening sky then vanish. She sings about the river which grows from beneath the hills where she has buried her memory. I follow her song into the hills where the air is deep and red and glowing and the sky is burning on our feet and tomorrow cannot be named. In the distance the hills embrace the sky in a horizon of slippery rays. The river grows from the sky.

I run because my voice is no longer me and my eyes are so filled with water. I run because my voice has fallen into a calabash inside my head. I wake inside a calabash where silence has no beginning, only death. Grandmother carries the calabash on her head and weeps. The river has followed Grandmother. She has brought the secrets of death in her mouth. I wait inside the river which Grandmother says begins in the mouth, begins inside the calabash, inside my tongue.

I hear a surging, violent falling, a thick cascade burying my song, in dawn and remembrance. I look for the joy in my growing. I long for tomorrow and daylight. I long for morning. I cry for Grandmother and she spreads her voice around me in a promise of birth. Her voice rises from her arms, like smoke, and I see the river which has watered our pain, which sings about all our belonging. A river is a mouth with which to begin.

It is morning. I find mother in my dream and I hear a knife, moving sharply, over rock.

Father . . .

Lemon trees. The trees are taller than the houses. Mornings and evenings are bright with lemons, a vivid yellow, a vibrant hue over the rooftops.

Our house is small, three tight rooms. On a silent hot afternoon a loud sound like hammering ripples across the roof. My ears echo a rattling sound. I search the inside of my ear with my small finger. I hear lizards running across the roof. I call for Grandmother.

A toilet is attached to the kitchen. They added it later, Grandmother says. She does not say who "they" are, but often she will say, They think we are animals. They make your grandfather work on Saturday. They make us suffer. They built the township. It is crowded in the township. I do not like it here. We live like bees. Who will bury us here? We will die like fruit falling from a tree. We shall bury ourselves. Shadows will bury us. We arrived as people, became strangers, share nothing but our suffering.

How can I cook on my palm? Grandmother says, exposing her hand. The palm has space for a fire, and a place to keep the dishes. The place for the dishes is a flat sink made of zinc, sloping into a hole in the wall where the used water gushes toward the toilet, then empties into the drainage. You have to be careful when you go to the toilet, there are always onion peels and vegetable stems on the floor. Sometimes it smells of rotting vegetables. I hate cabbages. A stoop at the kitchen door, four tiny steps made of cement, kept polished. I sit there counting, sometimes.

The stove is large, made of heavy iron. We use wood for the fire. We buy the wood from the township store. Across its forehead the store says, Goremucheche Trading. Grandmother says the wood should be free, after all it grows by itself in the forest with no one to help it but the departed. But they sell everything to us here, she says, they sell water. They have taken the water and hidden it somewhere. We open the small kitchen window to let the smoke out. We open the door too. The kitchen door is loose on its hinges. It creaks despairingly. We leave it open all day. Grandfather pulls the door when he comes from work. That door makes my ears sing, says Grandmother.

The tiny kitchen is black with smoke. Soot gathers in the corners of the room, hangs below the roof, creeps out of the crevices on the walls, falls into the food while we eat. The stove sits patiently beside the small window, squeezed at the far end of the kitchen. There is an oven too, with a small but heavy iron door: D o v e r. Grandmother uses a large metal hook to lift the door and place the food inside the oven. The stove is very hot.

From the stoop I watch Grandmother cooking. She calls for me to bring some wood from outside. I like bringing the wood. In the mornings I clear ash from the stove and carry it outside in an old metal dish. I throw the ash into the garden. It puffs angry whirls that climb into my hair. I throw ash into the hedge. It settles a gray cloud over the hedge, very quiet. I find a little piece of wood, only half burned, and I return it to the stove. Sometimes I find a red glimmer under the gray ash. Once exposed it burns quickly, and dies.

At night Grandmother leaves the door to her room slightly open, leading to the room in which I sleep. It is a small room. Most of the family furniture is stored here; a large table made of wood. The table fills half the room. There are no chairs around it. I can smell one of its legs while I sleep on the floor near it. It bears no cover or polish. That table has brought the forest into the house, she tells me. It smells like a tree. In the morning I fold my blankets neatly, walk carefully around the table, and place them in Grandmother's room. I am shorter than the table. When I have woken under the table, I think the house has shrunk even further. I crawl out and fold the blankets into a small heap. I sit on the blankets waiting for my grandmother. I watch my grandfather leave for work.

On the table sits a rusty sewing machine. Grandmother oils it, dabs margarine over it, polishes it with a small cloth held tightly between her fingers. She makes it run a few stitches, then the thread sulks and breaks. She mends an old dress. Often she just threads the needle. The thread moves through many different hooks before reaching the needle. Grandmother is very careful tracing the path. She bites off the end of the thread, smooths it with her tongue, rolls it gently between her fingers, then runs it quietly through the needle. She tries twice, tries three times. A ball of white thread sits at the top of the machine, turns frenziedly when the machine is moving. Across the bottom of the large black handle, in gold: S i n g e r. Sometimes I remove the cover very cautiously, my heart beating rapidly: S i n g e r. I run outside.

Grandmother's room is very dark, with a small window on one side letting in the sun. The curtain is frayed around the edges. Old, almost transparent, it captures shadows moving across the hedge, on the road. The window faces the road. Snap . . . snap . . . a sharp trimming round the edges. The scissors have an orange handle. That looks better, Grandmother says, to the curtain. The curtain leaves the bottom part of the window bare. Every morning, before the curtain is fully drawn, an oblong white light waits at the center of the room. I see it when I bring my blankets. I walk over it and the light folds into my eyes.

I stand still and the light grows warm over my arms.

≈

VaGomba never opened his eyes again, but fought the blindness with what he had already seen from the earth. He knew the earth and all the varying lengths of its shadows. Muroyiwa grew in this blindness which sought light. He was the last child of his father. He heard the details of this death from his mother who whispered to him around the cooking fire when there was no one else who would hear. Whispered about the fateful root and its ire of lightning, the forehead torn, its edges soft like cotton, the eyes swollen, the eyebrows pulled from their own roots by the drying blood.

VaGomba asked for his son Muroyiwa and touched him across the forehead. VaGomba would say, afterward, "You have grown." Muroyiwa would retreat from those searching fingers, from the entreating dark hum of the hut, and close his own eyes in imitation of his father's silence. He would try to recognize objects, without light, move toward them and touch them with recognition. He learned through this that recognition was something separate from sight, from understanding.

Recognition. An aspect of silence, perhaps more crucially of touch. It existed on the boundary between oneself and the world, between objects, animate and inanimate, rose thin like a coating of milk, equally tasteful, something you could feel on the tongue like an incomplete suggestion, the taste of smoke for example which allowed you to feel flame. Recognition made you feel you had skin separating you from air. It was something like that, to do with skin and bodies, and the abundance of free light. The absence of light could be central to recognition, the hollows of light, laden with silence. Muroyiwa lived in this chasm calmly willing his own blindness, his fingers discovering the hidden edges of things; the soft recesses of sleep, the sharp edges of hunger, and the rounded curves of water held in a calabash which reminded him of death.

His fingers sought the surface of water, not the water itself but its surface. There was such a thing, and when he held his fingers above the water long enough, the freshness crept coldly and slowly toward him, rose in the thin air that separated his fingers from the water, then he lowered his fingers by a single exhalation and touched something which clung to him, above the water, dry but soft like gathered dust, slightly sticky like honey. This sweetness was the surface of water not the water itself. Not water. There was a difference. He would keep his body resting there, as it was his body he was concerned with, really, more than his fingers. He would keep his body suspended on the surface of water, in that absent light, and this feeling was the tenderest. He waited in a wave of dusty water, soft, gathered from the tips of memory. He felt he had skin. He had woken from a burial pot.

Once he touched his mother's forehead and said, "You have grown." His mother laughed at him. When he was alone, behind the huts or away in the fields, he closed his eyes and listened to sounds that would reach him. He heard piercingly when his eyes were closed like those of VaGomba. He heard the air move over his young arms. There was something deep in the blindness of his father, something he could not reach even when he closed his own eyes all day till he fell gradually into sleep. Muroyiwa could open his own eyes at will, if something frightened him enough, a strange sound perhaps. This ability for choice his father had lost forever. "You have grown." His father mistook him for a root in the ground.

There was an intimacy of hostility between the root and VaGomba. Muroyiwa envied this intimate aggression, its attractive violence, and the mystery of something banished but permanent, the sound of death in a calabash. Death defeated sight, tamed it to a smooth forgettable memory. VaGomba had courage: Muroyiwa had sight.

Muroyiwa longed to find the root which harbored the sight of his father. One day this root would climb outward to the sun, grow, and bloom. The flowers would restore sight to his father.

∾

seven

Mother is turning into a single horrid sound, her voice beaten and lost, her shouts cowering in the midst of her dying. Her voice is crushed, turns into dust, rises in a piercing empty wail. The voice trembles with the end of life. A thin crying through dry crumbling leaves escapes toward me, calls desperately. The voice is wounded, limps sideways, hides. I remember the voice falling down twice, before a final silence. A door closes, very loud. The voice gropes in futile weakened sighs, and fades.

Mother has risen, after falling like that, grief-stricken. I remember her voice shattered, hidden, swallowed by the ground. She walks in wounded footsteps toward Grandmother. Her head is frighteningly bare. She has thick black hair held together by white thread in tight knots that pull the hair from her forehead, drawing at her eyebrows. The white thread twists through her head. Her voice is knotted, unable to breathe.

She wears a cloth which travels around her waist, over her left shoulder, under her right arm. It is tied tightly between her breasts, which are pushed cruelly apart, pushed to her armpits.

Mother waits, a wounded stillness, without words to help her waiting. Come inside the house, Grandmother says very slowly, very carefully. Mother enters and sits humbly on the bare floor below the wooden table.

Grandmother's face says many things to my mother, her hands moving here and everywhere saying many unspoken things which the mouth cannot carry, the things of inside, not spoken. She says the things women say when they have met each other in water, seen their faces in puddles of mud. Grandmother looks closely at mother and her looking is her speaking of the things they understand between each other, which they speak and speak, in their silence. Not a word from Grandmother.

Then Grandmother gives mother a large white cup full of water. The cup is white with a black rim. Her hand, giving, speaks and speaks, with the curve of its elbow, with its length and its grasp. Water is good, says Grandmother. Mother drinks. Her teeth are heard beating against the cup, her bottom lip trembles. It bears a red gash in the middle. It is swollen with the suffering which visited her. The cup has one large red rose next to the handle. Mother's knuckles, bruised, rest on the rose. She speaks and speaks with her drinking and Grandmother listens, moving her shaking shoulders forward to hear the unspoken things of her mouth. Mother drinks without pausing, and hands the cup back. Her movements are slow like sleep. She extends her right hand, and places the fingers of her left hand beneath her right elbow. She bows her head briefly as Grandmother reaches the cup, retrieves it from shaking fingers. Grandmother leans forward, her face broken, carrying the heavy things of life. A lonely exhalation, a deep silence. Mother has brought a lingering sorrow, a visit from yesterday.

Mother has spoken, but her face says her mouth is full of the anger which entered her, surprising her. Her face says she has found herself in a forest, lost and bewildered. Her silence, her shattered eyes, tell Grandmother everything. Grandmother shakes her shoulders in another grieved ululation. I have heard the blood in your voice, Grandmother sings.

Mother speaks in a quiet and sorrowful ululation, saying to Grandmother . . . Did he not teach me silence, this husband, that a woman is not a man? I am silent. Just silence to speak my silence against the husband who is not a man but a lizard with a rotting stomach. Like a hen chasing its own shadow he has left footprints which cover the homestead but lead nowhere. He has stolen the light of the moon and its promises of birth. He has thrown a handful of sand into the eyes of his clan as though they are nothing, turning them into insects, carrying everyone, the born and the unborn, in a wave of shame. He has prepared his own burial ground, when the ancestors have not called him. I will begin the spurning for them lest they mistake my silence for betrayal, so first I will bury him like a dog . . . I will not bury him but throw him away just like a dead lizard. Have you fed on the carcasses of dead owls? I ask him. Have you seen the sun forgetting its direction which it has known for many years, turning, in mid-noon, to go back and set where it began at dawn? Have you seen shadows repeat themselves, grow once more where they already grew in early morning? Are these the unmentionable sights you have seen? He has filled my mouth with decay, turning the tomorrow of my child into death, burying her, in the middle of the night. My child . . . her closed eyelids . . . her face wet with tears. I open my eyes wide into the darkness and search for my daughter but she is gone, she has been carried by a dark cloud and when she returns I ask, in astonishment, is this my daughter . . . Zhizha . . . is that the sound of your voice and your crying . . . Zhizha? But there is silence, the cloud has covered my daughter with ash and filled her mouth with death. Her brow speaks the mysteries of deep silent lakes. She speaks in a trembling voice which struggles to speak all the pain of her heart and of her growing. She speaks, in one mouthful of speaking. I embrace all her speaking, all her sorrow . . .

Mother has stopped speaking and looks at Grandmother. They stand together, looking at the things they have spoken. The things they have spoken are spread somewhere on the floor where they were seated. They look and look for them. They stand emptily, without words, and they do not tire of their standing. Their standing is heavy with the sufferings of the earth. Grandmother stands with her arms held over her chest, with an ululating shoulder. Their waiting is silent with no words to accompany it. The words have been spoken. The words have vanished.

Mother whispers softly, calling me into quiet . . . Zhizha . . . she says . . . Zhizha. The one who quiets me, the one who reminds of sleep, the one who comforts. Zhizha, a lullaby for my sleep and my light . . . Zhizha.

Grandmother cries into the night. She cries that the sorrow which has visited has no origins. It is sorrow which has no disguises. We are naked on this earth, she cries. Grandmother cries about the many words a woman must swallow before she can learn to speak her sorrow and be heard. There are no words only sleep and death. Death will always be waiting to relieve one of sorrow, she says. We have become strangers to sleep and our day has no beginning or end. Grandmother searches the night and finds her place of forgetting. This sorrow is like smoke which banishes the trees and the sky. She retrieves a single word, a word too heavy for her, a word which has turned her head white with suffering.

Grandmother finds the word and carries it between her fingers, and gives it to mother.

Tonderayi . . . Grandmother offers this word in circling cries. We met in water, she says. Tonderayi . . . she cries again. Grandmother says these are the things for forgetting not remembering. These are the sorrows of life, the sadness for burying beneath the earth, without words. Tonderayi . . . Grandmother cries into her palm which carries this one word from her mouth into our midst. Sorrow is like this, she says, it has no disguises.

We live in the township. Each crouching house is hedged. The people are hedged in. An arm swings in a wide continuous slash slicing the air and the hedge. The blade moves sharply downward along the sides, climbs swiftly to the top, moves sideways again, very quickly, then backward and up above the hedge falling downward, fingers chopped, detached, severed. Slash. I watch a short piece dive upward, turn and turn, fall blindly to the ground where a froth of milk forms, bubbles, is sucked by the earth. The milk is thick and creeps over the long wide blade, stirs, dripping awkwardly down. The hedge is stunted, parted, hewn. Milk bleeds white from the hedge, bleeds slow over the lush greenness, bleeds from fingers fresh and growing climbing upward to the sun, past dense branches, growing boldly, blindingly in a sullen milkiness. Cut cut cut. Milk drips to the ground, surrenders a violent purity. Bright white. Cut cut. Milk drips over a lizard and it darts forward, carrying the milk which flows quickly to its belly. In the brief distance it pauses, breathing hard, while the milk dries over it. Milk dries over its eyes, now slow and languid. The lizard breathes hard on its stomach, moves slowly toward a small jagged stone, waits with a limp tail. Milk pours in thick drops to the ground, along the hedge.

The milk in the hedge is bad, Grandmother says, pulling me away.

The hedge grows again. Green hedge with fingers of thick milk swollen and tender, in branches dotted with tiny angry leaves. I touch the growing shoots. They are soft with waiting milk. I break a small shoot carefully. I turn and find Grandmother standing, nearly hidden. She is singing in a low murmuring voice. I know she sings about me and my mother who have brought this loneliness to her. I press hard and the piece breaks from the hedge. Slash. I hear a knife move through the silence.

Dot dot dot.

White, with milk.

≈

Muroyiwa watched butterflies in the fields. The light poured onto their wings like milk fallen from the sky and they rose in a unison of lightness, in a combined breathlessness, and met the warm blue air spreading beyond the bushes of thorn which carried delicate yellow blooms. The blooms of the thorn trees were like feathers. Muroyiwa saw the butterflies lift from the field and move toward the array of flowering thornbushes where birds had built their nests. The cloud of butterflies swirled, rising like white mist, lifting like innocence into the air. They moved not far from the ground, caressed the earth in endless enchanting whispers. A distant mountain had opened and released them and their wings danced blooms of sweet light which fell through the shadows of the tall trees. The butterflies were all white, small like drops of rain. Tiny, they spread in an arc like seeds flung, strewn fervently into the air where they would not grow. The arc held them together. The sharp curve of their path fought a heavy wind which threatened to tear them apart. They danced a mute circle around this wind, then quickly and unexpectedly fell beneath it like dry leaves shaken from a tree, fell so near to the land it seemed they would rest there, but something imperceptible blew them from the ground and in an instant they rose, higher than before, and spread their growing arch sideways into the bushes. In a sudden distrust they paused, listened to the light falling eagerly on their wings, then together they whirled into the clean air. Their wings rising and rising and rising in a blur, in a shared sensation of fancy. Their song complete, they rested among yellow petals and thorns, their wings held above their bodies in erect and rounded surfaces, like fingernails. They waited stiff on their wing tips. The butterflies were solid and soft.

VaGomba continued to plant his own fields. He walked to distant villages. He walked faster than anyone in his village. Muroyiwa watched his father's brisk movements. There was something he had to gather from the dust and frenzy lighting the path. There was not much said between VaGomba and Muroyiwa, not much spoken. No instructions given, no expectations raised. VaGomba had no wisdoms to impart. He continued to plow the fields. Muroyiwa followed his father like a breathless shadow. VaGomba sought to heal time, not sight. It was time that had been wounded when he lost his sight, not sight. For healing he sought a rhythm of light. There was an arch that linked the morning and the sunset and he existed within that arch of light. With the arrival of dawn he rose and went to his fields, raising his voice whenever he discovered he had been the first to rise, before VaMirika, before any of his household. "Muroyiwa!" he would call. "Muroyiwa!" That was all. It was enough. It did not matter whether Muroyiwa heard him or not because the call had nothing to do with Muroyiwa, but it was suggested that if this child had woken from death why must adults remain asleep beyond dawn. "Muroyiwa!"

VaGomba cleared the path with a well-worn stick. He moved from one year to another capturing light, trapping it with what he accomplished each day, working furiously before darkness became intense. He felt the darkness descend over his arms like cloth, and his arms grew weak, and he could not work anymore. He felt the disappearance of light like a loss of consciousness, like thirst. He woke at dawn and the cloth of darkness lifted slowly, peeling from his arms. He woke in a fine thirst into the shape of the earth and treasured the sound of its stillness, not its quiet, but its stillness. This calm was its being there, his ability to move through it solidly in active anticipation of growth and of harvest. The presence of a life spreading from the dawn of trees and the clamor of birds at morning, was his. There was a stillness behind the clamor for life and a certainty belonging to him, which he could gather with his mouth and cry, "Muroyiwa!" He rose in the morning with the light, in the light.

Muroyiwa heard his name in the wind. He did not answer. He listened to the lightness of the wind which held his father like a net. "Muroyiwa!" The wind held his father in a swirling tightness. That timbre of a voice rising beneath closed eyelids, beneath the secrecy of a blind mask, excluded him but brought forth the miracle of his birth. He was birth, somehow, he was what had brought him forth. This truth of being part of an event thrilled him. It made him afraid. It surprised him that his father, in his blindness, was more possessed by this truth and that he saw more of the surfaces of things. His name meandered in the distances and floated with the birds at morning. His name was also a whip, a mockery—of sleep and prepared burial mats.

The secretion of light, to be the source of it. VaGomba accepted the light with his body, not with his eyes as almost everyone did. Muroyiwa could only receive light, not surrender it as his father did, no, not that. So he curled further into sleep and closed his eyes, blinded by the harsh voice of his father calling him. There was a point between the beginning of that voice and the end of it which he listened to, there was no voice to it, only the hint of something not said, a vibration, a touch merely. One of these positions belonged to him, the other to his father. Sometimes he imagined that he was the point at the beginning, other times at the end. Finally, he would open his eyes and watch the light enter the hut, penetrating the thatch. Light had a soft, gentle, determined way of gathering sleep from his eyes. There was a beginning to things, a point so small it could not be touched with memory, not felt, just spreading into the larger things that could be touched and felt. The end of things is also like that, a sort of vanishing which imitates the beginning, impossible to separate from the beginning except for its indescribable faintness. The beginning grows into something; the end into nothing but what has been. "Muroyiwa!" VaGomba dominated the beginning of things and their unquenchable lightness. He gathered death from a calabash and cast it like seeds to the wind.

∼

n i n e

Raised, her elbows speak the sorrows which her mouth has buried, which her arms have gathered and hidden, which her feet have harvested in their nakedness. Her arms sway in the rhythm of her silence.

Grandmother says how can we bury the pain which has visited us? It is deep and hidden. This is a tree whose seed has come from unknown lands. There is no water to banish it. This pain cannot be carried in the mouth. There is no mouth. It follows one like a shadow, this pain. It is hewn from rock and larger than memory. How can we carry it on our shoulders? It is swollen like clouds of rain. It is greater than all our yesterdays. It is lightning from a burnt sky.

A woman forgets her name of birth when she meets such suffering, Grandmother says. A woman becomes only a branch on a tree, becomes only a grain of sand. But do they not say even a grain of sand has a mouth to speak? Do they not say caterpillars speak with their many legs? Do they not say that butterflies speak though their wings are only made of dust? Do they not say that leaves greet each other in the morning? But a woman endures, becomes only a memory of all her yesterdays. A woman looks into her dream and discovers a silence with no wings.

Zhizha, Grandmother cries. She folds her arms and her hands along the back of her head where lightning has gathered and weeps. Her arms are silent with weeping, her memory old and far away, folded into some chasm in her past. The air is creased with the weeping of her arms. Tears caress the back of her fingers, gather beneath her arms which release all the living from her voice without giving her the freedom she seeks. Her forehead is unspoken. Her elbows are bruised from her mourning.

Grandmother searches beneath her tongue and finds a word to carry the sorrow which has triumphed over all her forgetting, which has found us. Her eyes seek the departed who have allowed this visit. Her eyes ask why the departed have abandoned our path. Grandmother stands in the midst of such sorrow, and weeps. She cries that she is surrounded by strange tongues. Something has entered inside her dream and buried her. I listen to the silence and death of her dream.

My back cannot stand again, Grandmother says. Our speaking has been stolen. Can morning arrive again into our midst? she asks, her voice longing and desperate.

I know that an unspoken word has arrived and uncovered this silence. I know the word begins with me. I hold the word between my fingers. I hold tight and the word grows deep under my tongue. The word cannot be forgotten. It has grown large roots among us. Branches sprout beneath the ground where memory is watered with death. This ground is stone but something grows on it.

Grandmother says that a woman cannot point to the source of her pain, saying, it is here and there. A woman finds her sorrow in her dream and everywhere. She is wounded even in her awakening. Sorrow is not like clay which is put beneath the sun to dry. It has no shape. It is only tears. Slowly she cries, slowly she weeps, sleeps, and wakes. Grandmother touches me with her word. I stand close to her and between us is the faraway place we have found, the place of abandon. Grandmother says even though we weep we wait to be remembered and to remember. She says if we wait till morning the dew will visit our feet. The earth has not forgotten us.

Grandmother's song enters into my growing and finds parts of me hidden and still and alone, full of the forgotten things of the earth. She moves nearer to me and touches me with her shadow. The shadow falls from her mouth, falls from deep inside her dream. I am swallowed by the shadow which grows from Grandmother and bends deep into the earth, lifting me from the ground, raising me high. It is warm inside the shadow. It is warm like sleep. I meet the sky in that warm place and the sky is inside Grandmother and it is filled with voiceless stars. The stars fall like rain from Grandmother's waiting arms which fold slowly over my shoulders like something heavy, sorrowful.

I wait for Grandmother to find me, to find all my dreaming with her lament, with her tears. Her song tells me about birth. Her song rises from ancient rivers where the sun no longer rises or sets. A woman will find herself in such a place where memory lingers like the sun, she says. In such a place women stand without trees to surround their weeping. A woman's cry is naked like birth, there is nothing to hide it. It is a place with roots but without trees. Grandmother's song finds the world where women gather. It is a place watered with tears. It is a place of remembrance. When the tears have become a river, morning will arrive even in such a place.

The river will become a tongue. Under the tongue are hidden voices. Under the tongue is a healing silence. I see the river. I see Grandmother. My hands touch the river which grows from inside my mouth, inside Grandmother, grows a murmur and a promise. It is true that a river grows in my mouth. It is true that a dream is also life. A dream cannot be forgotten, it grows roots where silence lingers. It is true there is a word beyond memory, fearless, gentle, full of buried worlds—a word licked with an ancient tenderness. It is true there is a word sweetened by death, lit by a fire gathered from a falling star.

A memory is a mouth with which to begin. We have no mouth, Grandmother says. Only the departed can speak our sorrow and survive. Only they can walk on a path covered with such thorns, such unwelcoming soil. Only the departed can celebrate the end of life and nurture death in a calabash till it blooms. Only they have a wisdom that can embrace suffering. Only they can gather, in laughter and dance, the brightness of the moon and turn it, once more, into death.

Mother.

I remember her unspoken sorrow lost and forgotten.

She killed her husband, grandfather says.

Runyararo . . . Grandmother calls my mother's name in the rain. Thunder breaks grandfather's voice apart, and I hear words drop slowly where he stands . . . dead . . . he says . . . police . . . he says . . . Runyararo. The darkness gathers. The rain has entered everything and made it wet. My hands are cold with the pouring water, with my growing fear, tremble with the cold . . . She killed her husband, grandfather says again.

A closing door, thundering loud. Grandfather walks briskly to the small kitchen holding his newspaper like a shield. He is going to read the

paper perhaps. It says M a s s a c r e in bold black print on the front, and
shows a man with wide shoulders holding a gun. The man killed someone. His eyes are open wide. He leans forward, out of the page. He wears
many leaves on his head in a frantic desire to become a tree. The leaves
cover his forehead, grow on the side of his face and across his chest. The
word of his mouth is twisted and angry, escapes through one side of his
face. Grandfather enters my thought speaking to Grandmother with a
violent flourish of his arms. He throws the paper into the fire. The man
burns. The gun burns. M sac e—the letters curl, curve, break, and collapse. The man loses his angry word. At the end of the thunder I hear a
single word, a gasp . . . the word hangs in the room, unable to sit or
stand, quivering.

A deep silence, only the rain falling hard on the roof like hooves.
Rain streaks the window in a furious descent. Falls like glass. I can hear
sheets of water digging somewhere in the yard. The mud flows round
and round the house, hitting against the walls. A thick gloom grows outside, spreading. I wait. Grandfather stands behind me. He breathes in
the rain, strains to be heard. I look away.

The lightning enters into something that Grandmother is saying
about my mother. I have endured, she says. What have I not suffered . . .
what have my eyes not seen . . . shall my eyes see more things of the
world? Grandmother came from very far, where there were rivers and
rocks. She does not complete her thought about the place she came
from, about her roots. She wavers and the name loses direction, darts to
a corner of the room, hides. Grandmother leaves the place of her birth.
She finds her present sorrow large and waiting. Something has dug her
past, torn her roots from the ground. She cannot remember the place of
her birth. Grandmother's hair is white with salt.

Grandmother places her arms firmly over her stomach and cries
about the sorrow which has entered our lives. Grandfather moves away

from her wish and her asking but she moves toward him, her hands frantic with her calling. She cries about anthills, tall anthills that fill the sky in a land full of dry rolling leaves and rigid grasses. She calls to the unborn, the forgotten, seeks the departed. She calls for her ancestors and her clan. She cries about the yesterday fate of her clan. Tomorrow is not to be known, she cries, tomorrow lives only in the mouth. She cries that she is lost, where is my clan and my people? she asks. The rain falls with the darkness, thunders across the roof, drops to the ground. Have you forgotten Tonderayi, she cries, Tonderayi who was here only yesterday? Do you think I do not know what it is to be conquered by a sorrow which has no name?

The black scarf falls from her head to her shoulders and she knots it again in one quick motion back across her forehead. The top of her head remains bare. An arrogant patch of white hair, exposed, turns her into a spirit which says do you want to see the things which are me, which have entered into my growing and my being? I have been burnt and destroyed and turned into ash but I have lived, even in my sleep.

Her hair is white with the things of the world. She tightens her scarf, moving in slow footsteps toward grandfather, hoping to be heard. Her eyes are bright with longing, bright with tears. Her voice has lost the long-ago places which are life. Her voice is stone. She cries about being a woman.

My words have lost their wisdom, grandfather says. He searches deep into Grandmother's thought and retrieves a segment of her sorrow which he rejects with a tall voice that says . . . You have stolen my words. You have pulled my tongue from my mouth. I have spoken and my mouth has been tied by a woman's wisdom.

Grandmother pleads to be heard. I have not spoken, she cries. I ask only for a humble silence in which I can be heard. You have said that a woman cannot speak. I have asked, is it well if I speak the heaviness on

my shoulders? I have asked if my woman's voice can be heard, small as it
is, is it not your voice too, does my voice not belong to you as I do? Can
a woman not speak the word that oppresses her heart, grows heavy on
her tongue, heavy, pulling her to the ground? I do not speak and my
word has grown roots on my tongue filling my mouth. Will my word
grow into a tree while I water it every day with silence?

Grandmother kneels, hands cupped, arms raised, head bowed, eyes
closed, shoulders limp . . . but grandfather says something about my
mother in prison, and Grandmother turns away.

Everywhere the wall is damp with the water.

∼

The only shelter for an insect is color, its ability to merge, to meet indistinctly, to exist without any flamboyance of difference. The guarded paths of ants leave serene traces on the ground, like faint whispers. Here, there are no remarkable footsteps, no phenomenal shifting of the ground, simply a peculiar disturbance easily forgotten. The quiet outpour of sorrow is also the strength of human beings, to leave no resounding echoes or footsteps, no memorable silhouettes.

The sweetness of secrecy became apparent during the war. Secrecy did not mean to hide, to be in a small place. It meant being in a naked place where it was possible to be found. One had to be unremarkable, somehow, silent as death. It was necessary to be inseparable, to embrace torture and despair and clouds of burning trees, to laugh a laugh that was also a fulfillment of fear. It was the similarity between voices that was crucial to living, to creating a landscape spoiled with fear, made pure with subdued desires. There was a chastity which surrounded its birth and a rigidity necessary to its completion, to its consecration. Not spoken, not loud enough to be heard, therefore not understood. Suspected, whispered from palm to palm, passed on to the young in sonorous chants. But chants are not words, they are part of the camouflage which buries words. Chants induce sleep and make mistaken identities difficult to discover.

There was happiness to hide the tears and more tears to hide the happiness: a lie to protect a truth, to tend an untruth. Insects survive during a war, creeping in careful caress, and for a temporary release and procreation, flirting dangerously in a spill of dust. In the tranquility of war those who burrow the earth in mimicry and pain, like insects, in a protection for life, possess the foretaste of freedom. From palm to palm.

Tachiveyi vanished. Muroyiwa thought of his brother disappearing like a point of light dying in the distance, swallowed by water perhaps, like the outline of a bird at the top of a mountain, like a stroke of good fortune, a stone fallen in water. In the ripple was a din of whispers and the repeated rediscovery of his name. He had died and if he returned home then he would have found another birth; in the ripple was the sound of the death of his people and an uncomfortable betrayal of their own surrender; in the softness of that ripple were their desires spinning in wider and wider waves, thinning into the edges of their sorrow, calling their names of battle. After he left, no one recalled the last words Tachiveyi had uttered, where he had last stood, the last meal he had eaten in parting. Details of his departure receded into the dark cloud that swept their memory to the sky. It had been suspected for days, for weeks, that Tachiveyi would be leaving. The restlessness could not be hidden, nor the triumph of decision. The excitement was like an explosion carried in his arms, for days, and he walked around wounded, healed.

Tachiveyi stopped working in the fields or helping with the harvest. His agony thick like flame, for months he followed the shadows, sitting at the back of the cooking hut, at the front of the hut, under the granary, behind the musasa tree, along the riverbank where the women brought their chatter and unwashed bodies. Tachiveyi sat amid their arduous whispers.

He carved a stool, which he gave to Muroyiwa. He had never made a stool before. He cursed and carved and worked in the dim light, mostly around the cooking fire. The flame burned sharply across his fingers and the edges of his knife, but his face was hidden. He tossed fragments into the fire, and bits of words he had chopped from his wood. He whistled a tune between clenched teeth. He made the stool in slow strokes of gray light. The stool was decorated with flowers. It held a lizard. Tachiveyi had removed the tail from the lizard and thrown it into the fire.

He would be gone for several days. He would appear, eyes dancing with the secrecy of escape. He had the eyes of one who is about to die or reveal a secret. Light spread an uneasy gloom in his eyes. Then without solace he left for the war and walked into its blinding black cloud, bleak and harsh. It was a bitter loneliness, with no illusions of a return but the comfort of his own mild sacrifice on the altar of war. An early death, this merging with the future, with the harmonies of war. Those who stayed home were also afraid, but they were outside the shell that contained those who fought, though this shell was thin like saliva.

∼

The house has swallowed death. It has swallowed the suffering of the world.

Green decay spreads through the walls. Curls of paint fall to the floor. Grandmother sweeps the floor with a tight grass broom. Rain creeps through the crevices. In the kitchen, the green has long disappeared, buried in the smoke. Grandmother cleans the house but the decay clings to it and spreads a gloom that descends into the air.

A bus comes to the township.

The bus rests on four enormous wheels. The bus says R O C in large white letters, bright white. The bus is larger than the houses. The bus is deep green, like the hedge, with one long white stripe splitting it. I call and wave as the bus passes by. Inside the driver sits in a deep green overall and I shout greetings to the bus and to the driver. I shout round and round, sing joyfully, turn and turn, fall to the ground, laugh at the wheels rolling and rolling so enormous. The bus driver waves and drives. He waves and drives.

Zhizha, Grandmother shouts, and I run back to the house. I hear the bus pass. I hear the other children run after the bus and laugh and shout, their voices disappear under the wheels of the bus. The bus runs over their voices. Zhizha, Grandmother calls, and I run toward Grandmother, toward her voice. I run.

I find Grandmother.

From the veranda, the air is blue, bright with birdsong. People pass by. Sell tomatoes. They collect shoes, repair them, bring them back. Sell onions. They collect empty bottles of cooking oil, in a small cart. The labels flutter in the hedges, bewildered. A bottle rolls from the cart and breaks loud against stone. It splinters, lies still, bright and jagged, in brittle disarray. Sell wood. A woman comes by carrying a wide basket on her head. It is afternoon, she says, it is afternoon she repeats more slowly as her shadow reaches us, bends, lowers the basket, kneels humbly beside Grandmother, delivering the basket to the ground. She removes a thin cloth covering the basket. She sells dried fish. Their eyes are glassy and blind. The tails are white, dry with salt. It is afternoon, she says brightly, and her shadow uncurls from her feet where it nestles, expands, swells with the basket, departs. Then a red round hat emerges slowly above the hedge, grows taller and taller till a man in a red-and-white suit shouts, extends one arm into the air, rings a heavy bell. He hands me a red ice cream. I pass it to Grandmother. She says no no and turns her head away.

Do I have a red tongue, Grandmother? I ask.

I touch my tongue.

It feels cold and still.

At night, the dogs bark. They have nothing to eat, but they linger. Their howls join in one pitiful crescendo, collapse. Their voices grow and mingle in the vibrating darkness. Voices chase each other up up over the roofs and trees, reduce the darkness into one resounding echo, turn and flee, spread a deathly chorus into the waiting sky. The song is broken, one echo falls on another, tumbles, dies, rolls away, hides in a distant silence. Then a frantic yelp, another effort to ascend, torn, horrid, like breaking bone. An angry call, like splintering rock. Voices circle, collide, race past the night. Then the voices find one more sustained rhythm, very brief, sink in one prolonged cry, very faint, scratching through the air. The township sleeps.

In the early mornings, anonymous voices proclaim the day, journey toward the city. Footsteps mingle along the tarred road. A man shouts. Someone calls back, running forward. The footsteps grow heavy, a voice tumbles forward, greets another, embraces, moves on. A voice runs in the opposite direction. A woman calls, just once. A thin simpering voice. Her steps light and quick. Someone laughs narrowly, in a brief cry. Steps move in a rapid panic, slow down, recover gradually as another reaches them, joins them. Voices welcome other voices. The steps move together, growing faint. *Hokoyo*, someone calls. *Hokoyo*, the voice calls on panicking feet. The word is lost, wanders searchingly through rushing footsteps. Later, a forlorn patter like dropping rain, reluctant, moving forward in chaste unhurried steps. Mingled with the footsteps, a voice sings a protracted sigh.

A heavy cough, then persistent spitting. Another harrowing cough, grating and abrasive. A voice digs through rock, surrenders day, surrenders night. Grudging footsteps turn and fall with a trembling hurried gasp. Footsteps approach, find the wounded voice, move sideways, step over it, move quickly past. The cough follows, pleading, trailing and circling a hollow silence. The footsteps vanish. An entangled halting cough, then the voice falling like rock, on rock. A slow rasping cough and the voice rises, moves slowly forward, to the city.

. Grandmother says my tongue can carry everything, even the sky. When I open my eyes there is no sky, only darkness. I must find the sky on my tongue where Grandmother says it is hidden, where my tongue carries it. I must call out the name of the sky till it returns, banishing the darkness. This is how the sun rises from under the land where it is buried. The departed call the name of the sky and their voices send the sky from beneath the earth, toward us. When their voices die, the sky departs from the earth. It is night. A stone waits in my mouth.

Grandmother says we cannot arrive far into our journeying if we do not surrender our tears to the departed. The journey is long, do not question it. When tears are so many even death can visit. Suffering is not death. Suffering can be carried in the mouth, not death. What has arrived cannot be banished like the footsteps of a hen which can be swallowed by the wind.

Women are children, Grandmother weeps. Our arms do not grow many like the branches of trees. We are children because our arms are so few. Perhaps trees dream of carrying many burdens. Trees have many roots but they do not have tongues to speak their dreams. Perhaps it is better to have many arms to carry your pain and no tongue with which to speak it. We have tongues. We are not trees. Our tongues carry all the memory of our pain. Our journey is watered with tears but we are not trees. Our arms are not silence. We know the way to the river even if grass grows overnight and covers our path. The path to the river is buried on the soles of our feet. This path has many thorns, but it is our path. This path is narrow but it is not death. Even the rain falls on this path, which is why the grass grows again on it. The grass does not grow on our feet even if we walk across swollen rivers. Tears have fallen on our feet and watered them, but the grass has not grown on our feet. Our feet keep many journeys. Why must we be silent when we are not trees? We have tongues with which to dream.

A woman cannot let her child rot on the ground. A woman is not a tree.

Women are children because they remember birth. If women are children, then children have tongues.

Grandmother pulls a word from her mouth and places it under my tongue. I feel fingers reach beneath my tongue. Grandmother's word grows and her mouth trembles with the word she has taken from it, that she remembers.

Grandmother touches my forehead with her tongue.

I touch my forehead and find the word Grandmother has given to me. I carry the word between my fingers. I know she has given me a word from long ago, a word that she has retrieved from an anthill. The word is covered with ancient soil, with all her memory. Grandmother buried a word in an anthill before I was born. It is a word that brings all our birth. It is a word filled with water. She buried it after rain had fallen for many mornings and nights. She buried the word to ease her suffering. When she had buried it she returned to the world and gave birth to my mother. Grandmother's arms are heavy. Her arms carry many words. A word is like a wound that has dried, she says. Runyararo, Grandmother says, giving me the word of her beginning. Grandmother brought this silence from a burial ground. The silence gave birth to me. Runyararo is my mother. My life began in an anthill where Grandmother buried one word and found another. Runyararo, she says. I know this is her word for burying the heavy things of the earth. I long to know the word which banishes silence, the word which follows her everywhere.

I see an anthill. Grandmother is inside the anthill. Under her tongue is a word. I wait under the tongue. I wait for Grandmother. If I do not remember the word I received from my own mother then Grandmother will remain hidden. I do not remember my mother. I must remember the word. I must remove it from under my tongue where Grandmother has placed it and return it to her. Grandmother has given me the word and I know it is a gift beyond life, beyond the known places of the earth, beyond all sorrow. My tongue is empty with no word to free Grandmother. An echo is not a word. An echo is the end of a word. After an echo is silence. I have swallowed many echoes.

Grandmother says a woman must not swallow her tears. A woman is not a tree. My arms reach toward Grandmother. She has given me a word which only a woman can give to another, give back to another. This is a place where women harvest. I touch this word and feel it on my tongue. It is a word heavier than the stone in my mouth. Grandmother says words are like that, sometimes one retrieves them from places that are forgotten, places that one has vowed never to revisit. Some places are long ago. When sorrow has visited, a woman will return to a place she thought had become memory.

A word does not rot, she says. It is not a fruit that rots on the ground. A word does not rot unless it is buried in the mouth for too long. A word buried in the ground only grows roots.

~

twelve

Three years after Tachiveyi left, Muroyiwa went into the mountains. He traveled to Njanja with a hope of encountering something separate from war. There was no rain in Njanja and VaGomba had stopped plowing the fields. He now carved stools. He carved many of these stools which had lizards with no lizard tails. He felt with his hands, and carved. His stools were more per-fectly made than the one Tachiveyi had carved.

Muroyiwa had heard that the war was intense in Umtali, that people did not plow their fields because there was so much dying, not because there were no rains. It was difficult to grow anything during a war, to tend something which had life and a tender root offered to the soil. Muroyiwa wanted to find something which was separate from the war. He would find it there where the war was.

It would be something benign, so harmless it would be impossible to miss, a feeling, perhaps, something he could touch. There was something unscathed, restorable, untouched. There was something mild as milk, mute, but not dead. A sound merely, a gesture from the sky, a singular sight. There was something.

He imagined his brother tearing off lizard tails, instead of fighting. He imagined flowers blooming amid signs of death and silence. Muroyiwa had never seen the mountains.

He arrived in the mountains and it was like falling into a great depth that seemed to alter histories, change an entire past. So towering were the mountains Muroyiwa forgot everything, particularly the war. It was the war which had a tender root to the ground, which clung to the mountains. Muroyiwa felt light and floating and insignificant. He was not important at all. He was trivial like an insect. He did not have a tender root to the ground, like the war. It did not matter if he continued living. The mountains had a life away from his own, separate and supreme. The mountains held him in a repose of sleep.

On the first day that he was there the mountains reached out and touched the sky with a smooth shelter of comfort, not death, those mountains swayed into the horizon, not death. The mountains greeted him in rolling green hills with feathery clouds descending, freeing those mountains which were high in the sky, and though the sky looked low and swaying, there was something like comfort held between the sky and the earth. The clouds were white and polished, clean with no memory of death. The clouds were clean like water. They washed over the mountains and released a pure light which lit the hills. Between the sky and the hills was light spreading and soaking into the earth. The hills were thin with the light from the sky.

On the second day the light and the mountains vanished. There was land stretching flatly into the wide dark ripples which met no sky, there was no sphere of light holding the edge of life, no horizon to nurture opportunity. There was despair, undulating like naked waves where the mountains had towered with simpler grace. The clouds were black and blew like blinding ash into the eyes. The clouds were powdery and swirled dust over the mountains, which retreated and shrunk into angry mounds of arid earth. The mountains emptied into the curling dark clouds which pressed insistently upon them, and the morning was dark and held a fierce magnificent calm. There was something like grief held tightly between the clouds and the mountains. The clouds tore and dropped into the mountains, then spread like a spray over them, like dry rain. No light just a tearing behind the clouds and they released the thick mist, black, which had the appearance of something crushed into a delicate pain. Muroyiwa held this black dust in his eyes, this black light which had unbearable grains of grief in it, then held his eyes together till he found the tender root which linked the war to the mountains.

The darkness swelled. This gloom made no sound as it fell and greeted the ground with dense layers of cloud. The dance of the clouds was a quiet release of fine dust pouring downward into these barren and bleak hills which waited, teased with the promise of morning. In the pale gray of this sky wrapped with gloom, with war, Muroyiwa stood blinded by a surging darkness.

The absence of light.

~

I dream of the moon. I dream of mother, Runyararo. The space is in my head, somewhere hidden. There is only one word kept safe in that secret place: "Tonderayi." I hear my grandmother say it. Grandmother carries the moon on her face, bright and lingering. Her eyes are closed. She hums a lullaby, about flowers opening, greeting the sun. The lullaby grows faint, wilts, dries up. She sits very still, and I hear her mutter, "Tonderayi." I take this one word from her mouth, pull it out like cobweb, and put it in a safe place. When she needs it I will take it from the safe place and give it to her. I keep it safe for my mother, too, because she says words are precious, like drops of rain, like milk. Words can heal old wounds. I remember mother, I remember her words. I turn to-

ward her, move close to her voice. I show her my old wound, on my
knee, a tiny scar.

The sky is dark and near, I can almost touch it, except I am frightened. A dark cloud grows toward me, above my head, moving slow and
near. It is carrying a lot of water. But it is dark, like smoke. The water in
it is very old, says Grandmother, the cloud has been carrying water from
yesterday.

My voice trembles, dries, beneath the cloud.

The cloud is full of waiting. It awaits the moment of birth, then it
pours water to the earth. The cloud is dark with promises to the earth.
The rain is dark in its promises of birth. Full of giving, Grandmother
calls from somewhere beneath the lemon tree . . . Zhizha . . . Zhizha. But
I see the dark of the cloud descend low and drop over my head in a slow
depression blinding my eyes and I shout down the tree and I fall, hard
on the ground, down on my knees. It is a long way down and there is
blood on my knee, dark red. Grandmother says,

Zhizha, do not fear the clouds.

I show mother my old wound. Mother touches my knee and says I
am too young to know of wounds. It is a bad thing to carry scars. There
are no words for certain kinds of scars, only sorrow and forgetting, she
says.

I keep the cobweb word I have taken from Grandmother's mouth. I
will give mother the word. Mother will heal her scars, her old wounds. I
will give her the moon to carry on her face, like Grandmother. Perhaps
Grandmother too will forget the word and I will give it back to her, perhaps I will free my mother from her journeying, perhaps she will remain
with me, perhaps I will remember the moment of my birth, remember
the way I cried, just like mother and Grandmother.

I see Grandmother bending, looking frantically around her, beneath
the bed where I sometimes hide, and I whisper, very softly, "Tonderayi."

She turns round, picks me up from the floor, holds my ribs tightly, asks very meekly,

What did you say, Zhizha?

Her voice is slow and searching, full of unremembered things. Her voice rises from silent worlds. I have stirred the cries of her silence. I have found the lake of her sorrow. Something has flown from her eyes, dropped from her chin, departed. I keep my silence to protect her trembling voice and her shaking arms. It seems to me that if I say the word again, she will drop me to the ground and die. Her eyes turn yellow with tears, and the skin falls from her face and dries up, all at once, like lemon peels left all day in the hot sun. I see her forehead spread into the edges of her face, as though something pulls at her from behind her ears. I see white hair framing her forehead, twisted, full of salt. Then I see her lower lip shiver, with tears. I hope never to see my grandmother look like that again. I am frightened.

I do not know if Grandmother remembers my face and my voice. I curl my toes beneath my feet and wait, wait to be remembered. The salt has left Grandmother's hair. It traces the top of my lower lip. I taste the salt on my tongue. The salt falls in drops from my eyes. I feel the salt falling. I do not move. My arms are still. I do not swallow the salt or Grandmother's cobweb word. I look at the silent shadow. I hope the shadow will surrender Grandmother soon. The shadow has swallowed Grandmother. Shadows are silent, carry many secrets.

Grandmother's eyes say she has forgotten me, that she has left the things of this earth. I do not cry. I hold the hidden word tight in my mouth and look at Grandmother. I long to know what it is that has brought this dryness to her face, this torment. I long to pick one ray of light and spread it across her forehead, but I do not know how. Then she places me helplessly, shakily, on the floor . . .

What did you say?

But again I resolve not to speak. I feel deeply that I have betrayed her. I turn away, knowing that she remembers me and the word that I have stolen from her. I have seen her hidden world, her place of forgetting. I decide never to give that word to my mother. I decide to take the word and hide it, somewhere where Grandmother will never find it again.

Grandmother stands under the green heavy leaves of the lemon tree. She stands there till the sky is dark and there is nothing left but the lemons going dot dot dot through the sky. I watch her, sorrowful, amid the lemons so bright. I wonder about my mother and my grandmother. I wonder about the places they have traveled. I wonder about the words they have given, hidden, stolen, for each other. Zhizha.

I touch the wound on my knee: my scar, my hidden world. I bend my knee and my scar widens and curls beneath my knee. I pass my thumb gently over my scar. I hide the word I have woven. Grandmother says I fell before I had learned to remember. When I was born my eyes did not know how to remember. After I learned to remember I fell down again, and my scars taught me to forget. Scars are our hidden worlds, our places of forgetting. I fell from a lemon tree. The tree had many thorns.

Grandmother holds me close to her breasts, saying, The things of the earth are heavy, my child. Zhizha, she says, very quietly. I listen to her silence and her dreams. I know then that I have the power to save lives. I never say that cobweb word, after that.

I long for silence. I long for the silence of mothers and grandmothers, their promises of a blissful remembrance. I linger, in my joy and forgetfulness. Grandmother tells me of birth, of the things which happened before I was born, before my mother was born. She tells me of her child buried beneath an anthill, tells me of her cobweb word.

Silence has endless roots. Grandmother gives me her word for remembering, for burying the torment of the earth.

Tonderayi . . . she says, her eyes held tight as they search. When pain is too much for the shoulders to carry, words become like dry leaves.

I remember your grandfather's words like uprooted trees, she says.

Your womb is rotten.

I married a womb filled with termites.

To remove the waiting from your grandfather's eyes, I waited too. A boy arrived into our decaying like one drop of cold rain and the waiting left the eyes of your grandfather.

Zhizha, birth is a soft cold touch like memory. Like drops of water on the back of the hand, becoming warm. Birth is like a beautiful feather wet with rain then covered with sun spreading once more over the palm, a blissful lightness tugging wondrously at the soul.

The birth of my son, Grandmother says into her memory, into me. I watched that drop of rain descend from the sky trembling and screaming, preferring not to reach us, not to surprise us. He never grew. He will never grow. When he arrived, all parts of him refused to grow except his head. His head grew and grew, a drop of rain that had lost the serene gift of flight, of its shimmering reflecting surface. I was frightened. His head grew with my fear, filled my arms and my heart and my song. They said his head was filled with water.

The water kept growing inside him, moving and turning, filling out into his eyes, in his dreaming places, silencing him. He will be gone in a week, they said, so gently. He will be carried by a river. You cannot save him. I cursed the Sabi the Hunyani the Limpopo the Zambezi the Mfuri . . . then I prayed to the departed for forgiveness. I turned from the wrath of ancestors and prayed for drought and starvation. I sent ululations to the earth, praying frantically.

Into his mouth I placed my breast, swollen with desperation, and he drank. I was afraid. He sucked the pounding of my heart and its rhythm. I would kill my own son. He would die from the pounding of my heart.

If you do that his neck will break. His head is too heavy. Do not embrace him. Do not give him a name he cannot hear his head is filled with
water his head is filled with water his head is filled . . .

So I knelt over him and fed him, and his head grew a growth so
magnificently painful. He sought the rain cloud that had brought him
from the heavens and separated him from a harmony where the silence
was an echoing of life. In the sky water-filled eyes saw with longing
where water and silence were held together.

Sorrow is linked to sorrow.

∽

fourteen

The butterflies were spread between the darkness and the light, each a round yellow which fit immaculately into the hand. The yellow was spotted with black drops and so the wings were stained with flame. Heavy drops rested on these fragile wings and pulled the butterflies to the ground but the yellow shone like something tossed and turning slowly with life. They flew near the ground and could not easily raise their wings. They moved in labored strokes gathering light while the proud spots spread on the wings which were newly hatched, and frail, and impatient with the desire for flight. The butterflies fell up into the sky and the spots were a multitude of darting insects captured in a net of vanishing light.

Runyararo noticed the butterflies from where she was weaving the mat, beneath the asbestos blue of the house which jutted to the right side facing the narrow street and sheltered her from the screams folding round the house from the back where the children played and cast spells on each other which made them drown. She could hear the rough stretch of their voices, harsh like maize husks. They clapped their hands to silence appetite, they made whistles from the hollows in their teeth and bit their lower lips to gather thought. They chased birds from beneath the roofs where they had built their nests and told them to fly simply because they could fly. Then regretfully they picked the eggs from the abandoned nests and held them well. They absorbed the warmth and secrecy of these perfect and harmless shells. They climbed back to the roofs and placed the eggs back in their nests and stood further away waiting for the birds to return, in vain. The birds, which hated disturbances and strange interludes, would not return. They failed to recognize the eggs as their responsibility, so they hovered softly in the sky, above the roofs, and swept away to somewhere. The unfamiliar scent the children left had wrapped a mystery around the eggs which the birds cared not to discover. They abandoned the nests and flew in cries limp with loss. Again, the children bit their lower lips to gather thought.

For Runyararo, the mat was like a heavy cloth that spread from her waist where she held it, over her thighs and legs, and nearly touched her feet. Her feet were bare. Her legs were curled modestly beneath the heavy cloth, the mat which was brown like the earth somewhere, not here where the earth was black clay and closely held like a secret. There was something missing in this earth, a certain softness that could nurture hope. This soil was dry clay but it did not matter, only lonely cries and hungry murmurs and insatiable hostilities flourished between the corroded walls of the small houses. Red roofs, yellow roofs, blue roofs. It was a release the bright colors the people spread repeatedly over these squatting shelters. The canopy of intermingling shades shone against the blue sky and tempted despair.

It was a wonder where the paint came from, how it was purchased or stolen, but it was shared like sorrow and held the people together. Holding hands without touching, this was it. It was not true to touch, not true to compete with clay below them which held tight and vibrating. From the rooftops going up there to the sky was a firm hope even if the rain had also disappeared and only the sun sent a brilliance over these roofs, there was hope because it was empty in the sky and they could each raise their arms up to trace an outline of opportunity above the roofs, above their heads, above their bodies because their bodies were part of a despair that did not rain, but flowed. Their feet were swollen through hours of factory work, their fingers blistered, their waistlines frail to forgetting. There was nothing down here on this firm clay except a trickling of desire caught between the tattered skirts of women who held large torn baskets over their heads and sold what they could, lived what they could. Dried fish, mostly, from somewhere where a river broke the earth or some water hugged the land. Somewhere.

The clean sky above, high and bottomless. They planted hope anywhere but in the ground where it should grow, they planted it in the sky. Down on the ground where they stood, there was just the dry clay, the children throwing stones, running naked, and splashing in the ditch water where the dead man had been found. The children had violent creases on their foreheads and swore at sunsets and anything which promised an ending; sleep, unwashed dishes, police sirens, rotting fruit, ripped car tires, disused houses, abandoned shoes, broken needles, fires, and farewells.

There were discarded bus tickets fluttering in the wind and stuck against the walls together with a few torn promises not yet buried, then the empty laughters feeding hunger, nourishing the desire to fly above the rooftops to that place free, clean, not anxious and tight like the clay which kept them captive. So they watched above their heads and waited while flies visited the ditches and licked the dead man's face, while the children laughed and licked the sleep off their throats then tossed cigarette ends which they had picked between the houses, tossed them over the dead face which did not remind them at all of their fathers. They had no fathers most of them, nothing you could call a father.

The township was a crumbling place with no edifice to it, no foundation but necessity itself. It had always been crumbling like any other place built without rhythm or consent. The houses were slanting, with no backbone to them. They fell toward the setting sun as though the ground had tilted forward to spill some long-kept hate out of them. The houses had been built for the workers at the nearby mine and at the many stores in the city center. Some worked at the factories that formed a shelter of dark smoke in the distance and others at the railway tracks which brought a trail of viscous smoke through the town and carried various goods. Some did not work at all but they stayed in this place and waited for something completely ordinary to appear. The township housed workers, not families. The people had been wooed from their villages into the township but others had been born here in the din of misery.

The walls of the houses had been painted white a long time back. Runyararo did not remember when the houses had been painted white and now after the years the whiteness had found kinship with the clay, welcomed it then freed it in grotesque patterns. The white had completely disappeared. Instead, it looked as though something poisonous had been spread like paste along the walls. A dog could be seen sliding weakly along a wall, and in the evenings, the smell of sewer water tumbling into the ditches. There was a smell strong with certainty.

Runyararo crossed one arm above another, her right fingers over her left arm which was scattered with dots of water that fell from the reeds she was weaving, she pressed the thin reed into a smooth needle and turned it into the waiting length of cloth she had already woven, along its edge where it would grow. Her left arm waited patiently while her right hand caught the thread underneath her left arm, under the mat, and she pulled it to a tightness that spread over the entire length of her left arm, and she felt the stretching along her shoulder and held the thread tighter still so that her fingers pressed hard again along the cloth she had created. Her right arm pulled the thread but first she dipped it once more into the small basin of water which stood to her right and as her hand rose toward her forehead in a tight arch that pulled the cloth toward her chest, the water fell onto her lap and across her left arm as she passed over it to meet the cloth. The water was warm and she did not mind it. It formed a comforting smoothness over her legs underneath the mat, the cloth she had woven.

The mat grew over her legs and she paused and stretched her arms. She released the something which had folded under her arms and upon her shoulders, a certain cloying tension. She felt her legs pull underneath the mat and she raised the mat and shook it away from her. It smelled like something old, something not easily forgotten. It had a deep smell which was different from the ditches that surrounded her, the ditches where a dead man had been found only last night. These small deaths did not surprise her. She had grown in the township and knew that the ditches harbored not just stale water.

Her mother had come from someplace where she had learned to sew mats. Her mother had taught her to sew mats. She said the mats could be made out of anything, even the plastic bags they found scattered in the township. It was the making of the mat which was important, the symmetry of mats, not their material. But sometimes

Runyararo and her mother found the true material for making mats, and this was a treasure to them. Then their fingers folded into the substance of memories. They bathed in the scent of an original place, a place away from the tight houses of Dangambvura where neighbors could hear each other snore, fight, and dream. Her mother said it was not good to hear another person dream. When Runyararo heard about the dead man she knew that he had died because he had heard another person dream. She had seen him. She with many other faces whose names she did not know. They all stood around the man till a police van came with a metal box and heaved him away. Runyararo wondered whose dream the man had listened to so well that it had killed him.

∾

f i f t e e n

Nights turned to water, a darkness wet with rain. I am afraid to listen to Grandmother, to discover her places of silence. I know there is a wide lake in her memory, a lake in which ripples grow to the edges of the sky, a lake in which all our grief is hidden. Her word rests at the bottom of silent lakes but she will find the word and give it to me. Finding the word is difficult and fills Grandmother with all the thorns of her growing. Tonderayi . . . she cries once more in her pain and memory. I hear my name carried in her voice. I know she will keep my memory safe.

Grandmother tells me of her son, of her hidden word, saying . . . Perhaps I had filled him with water at the moment of birth while he still slept. Perhaps my cry for help in that time of birth had confused his journeying and he had chosen not to be born.

All that water, warm, moving over my legs, joyfully giving. I should have kept him safe, inside of me. His head was full of water. He would never grow, only his head would grow. Place him in a clay pot and bury him. I did not listen to these voices. I waited.

I lay down in a bed of song seeking those ancestral places from which I would learn to part without regret knowing that death is also life. I had been given the gift of death and my method had been to feel scorned and humiliated in the company of my husband. He never went near the child. The child was my own mistake and I had to clear it up in my woman way, with the help of my own kin. One night I dreamt that your grandfather picked up the child and walked into a large thick forest, saying, I am tired of this waiting. He buried the child in an anthill in the middle of a dark forest. He buried the child without my presence, without telling me about it. The anthill began dissolving as though melting with sun, turning into mud. This red earth flowed rapidly following your grandfather through the forest.

Your grandfather drowned in that mud. His eyes turned an anthill red killed by his own son whom he had abandoned. For once, he asked me for help. He implored me to uncover my secrets which would save him. I offered him the desperation that had swollen my breasts. He preferred death. The child remained with me but the dream left me with a strong distrust of your grandfather.

His relatives whispered that the child's existence was evidence of my talent for untold evils. Who among them, they asked, was capable of such a miraculous distortion of birth, such a profound aberration? When they had finished retracing all the flawless histories of their births they shouted in one resounding voice saying that indeed, my powers would destroy their illustrious clan and I must be returned, immediately, to my own kin, with my offspring. Something stopped them. If I had produced such a miracle of birth, was I not capable of willing something similar onto their wombs? In deference to their own fates, there-fore, they retreated, still threatening, though in whispers which they made sure did not reach me. They disguised their threats into repeated greetings, but I knew all their natural and acquired abilities for life-denying exchanges.

He drowned.

There were always those who knew and said it was not like death at all, and I should never call it that, for he had never lived.

He has come on a visit, to see the things of the earth.

He has brought water in his eyes.

He is a semblance of life.

She is a digger of graves.

My son drowned one night while he slept. He drowned a fierce drowning. I buried him in the voiceless inside of my heart. He is the son of my ground.

Tonderayi. One who remembers.

I sleep, a sharp sleep like a piercing thorn, missing my mother and our belonging, crying in my sleep. Grandmother's voice comes and sleeps beside me. There is nothing to fear I am here, she says. Her voice is filled with milk.

She ties a scarf over my head saying look, there is my little girl. I touch the scarf on my head. It feels heavy and tight. I take a few steps with my head held high. I am Grandmother. The scarf falls off my head to my shoulders.

I wear her hat which she placed on my head one morning saying you are me, you are the one who is me even more than your mother.

She sings a lullaby rich with flowers, saying, rest on my shoulder and your face wet with tears so bright.

Her arms are warm with scented embraces lulling me to sleep. A small blanket folds neatly round my shoulders, round my neck, below my chin.

Sleep, my kind girl, do not be afraid, do not cry for your mother. Your mother is strong like the skin over your knees, touch the strength of your mother here on your elbow. I turn in a muffled voice saying there is only you, Grandmother. Mother is strong like the soles of my feet. I turn again from Grandmother's pleading, my tears spreading warm over my ears. Grandfather says we must not talk of mother.

Grandmother says I smell the earth under your arms and the rain smell. She remembers the forgotten things of the earth so old. Her brow is filled with promises of dawn, filled with the distant places of the moon she has traveled.

I see you, Grandmother. Where is my mother, is she dead? Grandmother gasps.

≈

sixteen

She walked through Dangambvura selling her mats, which she had rolled and tied together. She would sell at least one of them, before the end of the morning. She walked carefully between the houses and darted among the children who were throwing mud at each other. She saw that the mud had not fallen on her mat, and walked on. Runyararo knew Dangambvura very well. She knew all its sounds and smells, its missing shelters, its lingering anxieties; in the early morning the smell of cheap soap saturating the air, thrown out into the yard in the used water, the stinging smell of Lifebuoy and Sunlight which provided a penetrating welcome. The air possessed a clinging despair which breathed into her and made her knees fold, a bitter smell which made her rub the saltiness off her eyes and kept the tongue heavy and numb.

Then as she entered the yard she found a small dish, made out of empty cooking-oil tins expertly welded together, a container beaten to a rounded flatness. The dish was now turned over to dry. A tiny piece of green soap lay safely above it, to dry. There was morning with dreams polluted and doubtful. There was the rich smell of cheap lotions, green and thick and unapologetically present, with names like Girlfriend, Black Beauty, and Dawn. It was overwhelming, this smell of cheap lotion.

Later in the day, the soap was swallowed by the ground and vanished leaving only a faint acrid touch to the air, and peculiar shapes on the ground where the water had dried. Entering in proud swells was the smell of onions cooking in oil. The smell of onion mixed with paraffin. A slightly open window released the paraffin into the yard, into the winding streets, and it had a taste to it, of frying onions. Paraffin that you could taste, the smoke in it, the folds of sadness in it, the onion in it. It sparked the appetite because it was food and made one remember though not really want food too much because it smelled like soot gathered in the mouth, like something poisonous wafting into the air, breathed and kept, this paraffin and peeled onion.

Dangambvura was reeling with improbable desires. If not the paraffin then the fires outside and a woman bending over a small pot using the bottom edge of her skirt to hold the burning handle of a pot. On such a predictable afternoon the onions mixed with the fire, cooking and tasting of flame and smoke. The smell of burning onions because the fire was too deep with flame and burned the onions and the oil, but this was food. And cabbages boiling too. Boiling and spoiling the afternoon with a smell which had the familiar morning scent of discarded soap in it. A constricting smell, suffocating. It was not good, this smell of boiling cabbage. It had a dulling feel, strong with something in it that made the head heavy and turning, something which was cooked to over-ripeness. It was unbearable this smell of boiling cabbage in these narrow streets patterned with stale voices where something else, other than faith, had been resurrected. A whisper of fatality or something equally complete. The windows opened wide, the voices thin, the desires louder than memory. Such were the ceremonies which nurtured Dangambvura.

Sometimes there was a new detail added to a house Runyararo had knocked on before on a day when she had been again selling her mats. This transformation was an attempt at restoring something lost and no longer recognizable. She saw stones placed in a straight row to surround a growing peach tree. She saw that a hedge had been cut, trimmed to evenness. A doll discarded, the hair golden and still shining, its eyes turned to the sky, its arms missing. A discarded wheelbarrow, the metal rusted, with an abandoned litter of cats fallen asleep, not interested in hunger or affection not proffered, not interested in their own abandonment at all, they simply slept while every curious sound visited every emptiness but their own. They slept steadily. Then a burst of peach blooms.

Pink and soft in that dense and dark place, a pink glorious spray of light blossoms floating and endlessly falling. You could pick the color from the ground like a dream. So tender and trusting, this spread of color, it made you hope and feel indescribable passions, it made the mind clean and hopeful. Such a sensation of simple bloom. When they fell the ground scattered with ephemeral light, tantalizing like quiet rain. Runyararo liked the fragile smallness of these peach blooms. She liked their promise of growth. They were pale and frail and polite. They touched the ground with a soft paleness, fleetingly. When the sun fell more solidly into the blooms they became thin, almost white with their glow, but when a cloud passed over the sun they became heavy and bloomed afresh. Something would grow on them, the strong blooms which remained on the tree and spread daintily over the branches.

Runyararo could already feel the delicate fur covering the skin of the fruit, not yet ripe. The pale green of the fruit, the narrow oval shape hidden beneath the deep green leaves which she liked to crush and bring to her face, briefly, just to remember the smell of peach leaves. The small fruit growing, even that she liked to open and discover the white seed inside, so large and so penetrable she could crush it and peel its whiteness off like a thin membrane. A bright white of seed that she liked to look at and know that in a few weeks it would have hardened, grooved, and changed into a solid brown. Only then would the fruit continue to grow, larger, itself hard, harder, then it would succumb to the sun and reflect some of its glow, sweeter, breaking into a tender yellow and faint redness, a smell so good it enhanced the sun and made it new.

The ripe peach split in half and you could see the brown seed inside the fruit because the fruit had matured and flowed with readiness. The brown hard seed which contained all the life of the tree in it. The ripe fruit, so soft when you pressed upon it and the juice ran freely through your fingers, and when it dried, left a sugary stickiness. It looked to the ground, the fruit, split in two neat halves that held together like a question. It desired to fall to the ground and rot there with its forsaken but cherishable ripeness.

Such a tenuous glory, this blossoming and ripening. Then the multitude of magnificent pink petals would be forgotten. Only the smell of ripening fruit with its mellow tint persisted.

~

This is the sea.

I pull the crumpled cloth tightly fitted into the mouth of the bottle. The cloth unravels and lies open. I smell the water. I dip my finger in the bottle and taste the water. It has a strange taste, like salt. I spit it out and wipe my finger against my flowery dress. I taste it again. That water can cure anything, Grandmother says. It is full of the things of life. The sea is large like the sky, she says, there are people who live at the bottom of the sea. They are good healers.

Grandmother does not drink from the bottle. She waits. One day she will grow very sick, she says, and die. On that day she will drink from the bottle. She will carry with her the things of the sea in her stomach, she says. No, I say loudly. I think of fishes and reeds. I shout again, breathing in water, saying I have swallowed the things of the sea. I see reeds swaying. Salt in my crying and in my dreaming. I hear the cracking of rock and the sound comes from the reeds, somehow, comes from the water dense and dark like stone. The sea heaves a large wave over me and I hear water breaking rock, crashing into eyes so still. The water climbs high, spreading wide across the horizon. I see darkness and cloud. No one can hear me shout. The darkness has closed my eyes, stopped my crying, covered me with furious sleep. I close the bottle tight with the cloth. I wonder about the sea. I see the people who live at the bottom of the sea. I see their shadows meet me, greet me, walk away in silence.

I listen for the voice of my mother, which calls to me saying, I remember the moment of your birth, you cried in a voice like mine, like my mother's. I listen and feel water move into my ears and close my mother out but she reaches a searching hand into the darkness and finds me, saying, I have seen you, my daughter, I will always be near. I am in your voice, in the sound of your crying. I am here in your growing feet. I have seen you, my daughter. She places her palm over mine and says I am here beside your dream, in the dream growing white on your fingernails. I see a dream grow a brilliant white wide across my fingers, and mother says do not be afraid, my young one, Grandmother is here, she is our tomorrow. I close my eyes to the rhythm of her beseeching voice crying in my sleep, then I speak, saying something soft into the night. The night brings my mother into my sleep in showers of slow rain bright and clear and I speak again, comforted.

Zhizha, I hear my mother calling in my sleep, Zhizha.

I cry to my mother frantically, saying, I remember my forgotten world. I remember the pain in my growing. I remember my stolen dawn. I cried in the voice of my mother and my grandmother. I remember my hidden world . . .

I run outside to pick the lemons which have fallen to the ground yellow and ripe. I pick them till my hands are full of tender yellow rays.

I turn. I see mother, her face covered in dry grass. Black-winged ants travel over her arms and her eyes in neat rows that weave into tiny circles which grow into each other, widen over her stomach, whirl and turn in frantic silent steps. The ants hurry over her face, linger over her with rounded eager heads, red, with white transparent sacs. They journey with a hunger, delicate and blind over my mother, climb triumphant, pour out bravely. Mother is still.

My voice falls from the sky.

Mother saying in a measured voice, Repeat after me

a e i o u

Diagonally opposite the dressing cabinet is a window and through it the sky, trees, and neighbors enter the house. Through the mirror birds fly past, sometimes.

a e i o u

I sit very still, reading aloud, repeating after my mother through the mirror filled with our calm resemblances and our hope, with sonorous song, with the quiet rhythm of our sleep, with the sound of my growing. I have discovered my mother's presence, her embraces and ululations of joy. I have found the moment of my birth, of our beginnings.

I have seen my mother.

She moves forward, hands me something held tight within her hand, the secrets in our belonging. We have begun our initiation into each other's worlds, our profuse illuminations. We belong and belong. Our yesterday partings vanish like unremembered dreams, like echoes of stream water, lapping gently. My mother.

a e i o u

I repeat silently. I repeat into the deep of the mirror far where my mother's eyes meet mine. I breathe a warm cloud over the shiny glass of the mirror and write one letter across it. I watch it disappear into the mirror. I breathe again another warm cloud onto the mirror and write the second letter, and again it moves away silently, slowly, and the mirror waits. I meet her gesture of endless warmth, her brilliant growing love. I meet the radiance of her eyes, and in her tears, I find my past.

I meet her in one motion of elation, a cry like joy in which she, in one tranquil turning, says, I have seen you, my daughter, I have seen the beauty of your earth, of your growing naked feet. I have seen the eternal worlds between your fingers and the secrets in your sleep, I have heard your laughter and its promises of dawn, I have seen the morning on your forehead and touched your restless hope, I have walked quietly in your sleep.

Mother calls to me in a voice just like mine, she grows from inside of me, saying rest your forehead here on my palm bright with longing, sweet with cherished touch. I have seen you, my daughter. I have seen into your dreaming, my loved one.

She gives me the moon saying the moon is in my growing and my sleep. I look far into the mirror and the moon travels silent and whole, breaks into small fragments, scatters to the ground in showers of joyful light.

I watch myself through the mirror, my mouth moving in different directions with the letters, my lips move forward when I say u, and sideways when I say e. I like most to say o, my chin moves down, the sound rises from deep in my throat, my breath a sudden stop so near. I sit beside the mirror. I repeat the letters carefully. I say the letters with my eyes closed. I close my eyes tight till tears fall down my cheeks. I feel them tumble, fall, and wet my lower lip. I open my eyes. I write the letters across the mirror with my finger. I paint them in blue ink, red ink, green ink, turn them into cloud and sky. I write and write over the mirror. I write downward, curling the letters round and round. Then I write quickly. I try writing with my left hand.

I sit up straight like my mother, my hands folded across my chest and a frown on my brow, and sternly say repeat after me a e i o u, then I change into me, and I say a e i o u. I remember all my letters. I tell my mother and she repeats after me and I laugh then I repeat after mother who repeats after me and I after her . . . I have turned into mother, and she laughs, because she has become me. The letters flow from me to mother.

My mother's voice is resonant and searching. She says we live with our voices rich with remembrance.

We live with words.

∾

e i g h t e e n

Runyararo and Muroyiwa shared a small room in Dangambvura. Their room was divided into two indistinct spaces by a short
fraying curtain. The curtain had large blue stars on it that were
faded and torn. A hard string ran through a seam at the top of the
cloth, and collapsed at the center where it carried most of the
weight of the cloth. On each end, on the wall, a small hook, with
the wall around it broken, held the cloth weakly. The cloth did not
reach the floor on either end of the room. One half of the room
supported a small bed, which was squeezed along the end of one
wall. It had a cream crocheted cover. It had large holes through
which you could see the heavy gray blanket beneath it. The blanket was deeply laden with coarse thread. The prettiness of the
cream cover mixed uncomfortably with the coarseness, it hugged

it tightly. The cover also was worn, especially around the corners where it folded over the bed, where it followed the bumpy angles of the mattress and was tucked carefully beneath it.

The bed was made of iron and stood very low near the ground. Some shoes showed under the bed, red women's shoes, a black pair belonging to a man. A brown suitcase with its plastic handles missing had been squeezed to another end and held more clothes that were neatly folded together. The suitcase had collapsed in the middle. The lid was almost torn. When it was used a long strip of black rubber was tied over it. There was no window on this side of the short red curtain with the fading blue stars. Nothing separated the two spaces but the hint of separation, the attempt alone.

The two pillows were very flat with use. When Runyararo and Muroyiwa did not sit on the bed, they took the pillows and used them as cushions to protect themselves from the cold cement ground. One pillow was held inside a torn black blouse. The pillows were hid under the laced crocheting. At the head of the bed, at the corner, were the mats Runyararo had made. They were rolled together and leaning against the wall. A small brown mat had been spread on the floor near the bed, and it was new. It was very neatly made, with pale cream stripes along the border, and deep brown circles at the center.

There was a solid darkness throughout the room, except at night when a candle flickered through the closeness and made the place whole and discernible. Then the shadow of the bed leapt onto the wall and made the bed larger, and the flame from the candle seemed to rise from the bed. The bed grew and rested angrily on the asbestos roof. The shadow of the mats leaning against the wall split the room much more than the curtain. The shadow was broad. It cut the room diagonally. The candle shortened, then burned low, and the shadows grew still larger till they vanished with the dimming light. The smaller light made the shadows round and flat, not sharp and peaked like the blossoming flame. There was light in the night because the candle was put to burn, more light than there was in the day when there was sun outside but no window to let it in, only that on the other side of the curtain was a small opening, which often was covered with a sheet of cardboard to keep out the ceaseless footsteps. The people passed very near the house. The shoes underneath the bed, the worn suitcase, stars falling off the curtain, and no light. The smallest light provided a moment suspenseful and empty. The light died. The day vanished with the light.

On the other side of the curtain were the cooking utensils. Runyararo did not cook inside the house. She cooked behind the house where she made a small fire between three solid stones. She brought all the pots into the house even before they were washed. It was a distance to the communal tap and she saved the clean water she had collected for their baths in the morning and for their cooking. The morning began with the dishes from the previous night being washed. They were made of tin, painted to a pale green, and hit against each other in the small bowl in which Runyararo washed them. Runyararo washed the dishes every morning while her husband still slept.

≈

I call for Grandmother but my voice sinks, disappears. Mother comes forward with tears in her eyes, saying, I am your mother, Zhizha. She stands still, looks into the dark trying to find her mother.

I see mother. She has come to visit her mother and to be mother. I see Grandmother. I see mother.

I watch her mothering strange as her visit waking me from sleep. I am your mother, she says, while standing at the doorway. I do not remember her face or her voice. I have forgotten my mother.

I have my Grandmother, she is my mother. My mother is away, very far away in the mirror, inside the house.

Mother laughs and asks to see the mirror, asks to meet my

mother. Anger creeps into her eyes like dirty stream-water, marring the
rhythm of her visit. I turn away.

I know she is my mother. I do not recognize her. I long to ask her
about the places she has visited, that have visited her face, but she hides
her tears, raises her shoulders high, and walks through the door, past
me. I follow slowly behind her. She turns away, moves to Grandmother's
room, sits on the chair beside the mirror, and places her face in her
hands. I enter the room, quietly, and wait.

I have been here all the time with you. Mothers are like that, she
says, they can never be away from their children. I can see you even
when I am not here. I am your mother. Nothing can change that, not
time not distance not even Grandmother. You are me, she says desperately. We grow together even when we are apart. We belong together. I
gave birth to you, my daughter. I heard your first cry. You called me
when you were born. I touched you in your moment of birth. You cried
and cried in a voice like Grandmother. You were born at dawn. You cried
for me and for Grandmother. We held you close. You are strong, Zhizha,
you are my daughter so strong.

You have forgotten your mother. It is like that with forgetting. It
does not choose this, saying no, a mother is not to be forgotten no matter how long her absence. Forgetting just comes and takes away everything. Some things are only suffering, it is not good to remember them.
To remember them is death. I think of you in your growing. I think of
my daughter. I am your mother, Zhizha. I held you after you were born.

I heard you cry in a voice just like mine, just like Grandmother. I
had not expected to meet myself in your voice, meeting my own mother,
meeting you, my daughter, all in one moment. I said to my mother,

Zhizha will never forget me, she carries me in her voice, how can
she ever forget her mother?

That is how it was when you were born.

I move back from her pouring words. I am not complete without possession of her memory and her desires. Her voice searches through me. I find a dim spot where I hide, and watch.

Her visit is a fragmented togetherness, a handful of caress like blinding noon dust. Her voice reaches me, lulls me to sleep. I grow toward her voice longing for her to stay, to give me the secrets of my growing.

I long for remembrance but a darkness grows on my forehead, buries my moment of birth. Mother's voice rises, troubled, toward me.

Zhizha, she calls. Zhizha, she calls again with longing. I long to shout . . . Mother . . . Mother . . . but something stops my crying, something in my throat. My voice is dry and lost. I sink back into sleep, waiting for my mother.

From one dress into another she seeks her profile in the mirror and smiles gently at me. I watch her beauty and her grace and her glowing long legs and bare arms and long smooth neck. I see my arms around her neck just like she asks me, and my heart beats fast, my heart is running away from this eternity of embrace, round and round. Then she turns, suddenly, dropping her garment to the floor and saying to me, Look at these breasts from which I fed you.

I look at her breasts. The tips are shriveled, like dried tomatoes, the elongated kind which droop to the ground and ripen in a sudden fury from the top down. I do not want to remember my mother. I think of red broken tomatoes. I think of milk, white and bright, from my mother's breasts. I think of ripe and red tomatoes.

She reminds me of my feeding as she moves to follow my turning face. It is all right, she says, I am your mother. She is so certain about giving birth to me and about my part in it. She cries at my forgetting, at the things I cannot remember. This is your milk, she says. I want to give you the things of your growing, the joys we have shared.

A tear falls onto my forehead and I stop turning, surprised, but she has returned quickly to the mirror mirroring us and puts on a red-red dress which she says she would never wear if there was lightning in the sky, for she would die so suddenly there would be no moment for remorse or forgiveness, and with that threat she leaves the room, calling to her own mother, and I am forgotten, for now.

Alone. I try hard to remember everything that has been because that is my gift to my mother. I move toward the mirror and pick the discarded garment from the floor raising it to my shoulders holding it against my flat chest seeking my mother in me, wondering about being a woman. I put the dress over my head and it falls over my body, folds around my feet. I stand looking at the mirror and my mother comes and stands behind me.

≈

Runyararo woke very early to sew her mats. She would sit in the half-light of the morning while her husband slept. She liked to work in the morning with the early light. There was a soft light over the houses. There was silence, except often a dog barked, something was heard falling, but there was a kind of peaceful light that surrounded her in her work. She felt the light on her fingers as she worked while sitting beside her stoep. She would have left some water in a small dish the previous night, and this water would have a strange coolness to it that she liked. There was a soft milkiness to the water because it was early morning and some silent smoke had grown over it. She would dip deep into the basin and her fingers tingled with the smoke, and then she would dip her reed in the water too. If she left a bundle of reed in it there would be a certain scent to the water that she liked. This was morning.

She thought of her mother who had taught her about making mats. Her mother lived not too far from her, only a few streets away. Runyararo was sure that she sometimes could see the smoke from her mother's morning fires because her mother was always one to rise early like herself. She liked to stand on her stoop and gaze into the distance thinking of her mother. Her mother had not been happy about her marriage to Muroyiwa but because she was already expecting a child her mother had relented. It was not clear to Runyararo what her mother disapproved of. Perhaps it was that Muroyiwa said he had come to the mountains to look for butterflies. This was not a good revelation to her mother who said a man could not travel from Njanja to Umtali to look at butterflies. It is the war he has come for, Runyararo explained. That is even worse then.

He had said his brother was in the war and he would no longer return to Njanja. He would remain in the town of Umtali and be near his brother. He said strange things about his brother tearing lizard tails and eating them. When he was really happy he told her about the different calabashes in his home in Njanja. Runyararo liked to hear about the calabashes, as there were not many in Dangambvura. He said he would take her to his village to see the calabashes. Then he said he had been born in a calabash. This was strange for her to understand but she believed him because he said it with such seriousness. He focused strongly on his birth. Runyararo was happy about this because she was having a child. She liked to listen to him talk of his village because it was a life separate from her own, and listening to him was like traveling to a distant land. She had never left Dangambvura. She had not seen the mountains Muroyiwa talked about, where the war was, though they were not very far from where she lived. But there was never enough money for an unnecessary bus ride, and there was a lot of fear surrounding the mountains, so much sacred ground, and the war.

Muroyiwa had found work in the mines and Runyararo liked that her husband held a job. They could at least have their own place to stay, not as crowded as the other homes around them, where two or three families lived in suffocating closeness. They had a large room and some privacy. There were few men who could find work. Muroyiwa had found work very quickly. The mine owners always preferred people who had not been born in the towns, as they would accept lower wages and work longer hours and be scolded without ever retorting. The people from the rural lands were considered to be good workers and the mine owner was willing to release a worker he had kept for a while, because he had stopped being grateful. So an enmity was built between the town dwellers and those who had just arrived.

Muroyiwa worked all day in the mines, digging at the rock beneath the earth. It was daunting work and there was always the fear of accidents there, disasters larger than themselves. This they tried not to remember or discuss, till something happened, till a roof collapsed and no one was rescued from the rubble. It was strange that the death was so far away and they could not see it or touch it. Then they filled the evenings with fears which would burn their lips for weeks, but they would return to the mines and work, their eyes black and dry with surrender.

In the evenings Muroyiwa would watch Runyararo creating her mats. She liked to work till the evening light vanished. She would sit outside and he would sit with her. He sat on a small rock which was held to the ground very near the stoep and touched the wall of the house. She liked his face with the gold of the dying sun, and he would watch the perfect symmetry of her mats, the confident movement of her arms, of her wet fingers, of her lips. The symmetry of mats between her fingers

gently folding, caressing every thread. She would pass the wet thread between her lips to soften it and recover memory and they would both be
quiet with no words spoken. She would twist the thread of reed between
her second finger and her thumb, rolling it over and over till it was thin
and taut and sharpened, then pass it through the thick braids of the mat
she had prepared, and hold the braid close to the place she had linked it
to, her thumb pointing toward her chest, and the mat held secure near
her breast like something precious so she could examine her thread,
what she had created; the symmetry of mats. She would spread the mat
on the ground and flatten it, her eyes moving devotedly over the cloth,
she would touch every part, searching, removing loose threads, pressing
away at the unevenness. She would touch the mat with a particular satisfaction, then look up to the dying sun. Muroyiwa wondered at his own
curiosity and pleasure, at the symmetry gathered in her face, in the moment they had shared; her wide smile which welcomed him, her eyebrows almost touching and thin like a clean mark on the ground. A
perfect shape.

Then the pounding in his head grew to a hum that would only return the next day when he would arrive at the mine, and there was silence in his hands, away from the breaking rock, from the darkness in
the mines. He hated that darkness he entered with his entire body and
which stole from him, descending, unable to breathe. When he swung at
the surface of the rock his forehead filled with the tremor of the earth
and the searchlight on his forehead dimmed. The light on his forehead
searched the surface and found it bare. He was an insect with a single
antenna held to the ground. He burrowed the earth with the light he
carried.

Returning to the surface of the earth made him free. He always
thought of his brother Tachiveyi who was in the mountains. It was his
freedom which his brother fought for. He was not ashamed to think of

his brother because he had followed him. He felt that he now almost lived with him. It would not be too far to visit the mountains again. But the road to the mountains had been closed. It had been named the road of death because so many people had vanished there. Muroyiwa felt fortunate that he had ever been able to travel there. It never occurred to him that perhaps his brother Tachiveyi had now been killed. If he allowed this thought to carry him, then he would lose his own importance. He existed as an opposite to his brother, the war was an axis which kept a balance between them. Tachiveyi had courage, Muroyiwa had stayed behind. Tachiveyi was the first born, Muroyiwa was the last. Being born last, it was Muroyiwa who had stolen the light from their father, VaGomba. Tachiveyi had created the milk which they had both received from their mother, Muroyiwa had dried it. Tachiveyi was at the beginning of things, and Muroyiwa existed somehow at their end. The return of Tachiveyi to Njanja would bring sight to their father. Muroyiwa never doubted that his brother would return. Each time the lift from the mine brought him into the light, he removed the torch strapped across his forehead and remembered that his brother too would return. This was something he believed. Muroyiwa waited for Tachiveyi.

～

t w e n t y - o n e

I hear something crushing under my rib like eggshells where Grandmother holds me and it is painful like the loss of my mother. I hear mother calling me, her voice is small like mine. She turns from the mirror to look at me saying, I have seen you, my daughter. She laughs. We met in water, she says. She calls to me again. I stand close to her sunlight, close to her. I wonder about opening my eyes, about touching the edge of her face. I see her smile blissful with our tender awakenings, soft. She enters my thought and says she is only your grandmother not your mother.

I cry with a delicate longing saying I want my grandmother who smells of lemon rind. I run. I climb up the tree filled with thick green leaves and thorns where I hide. When I come down my mother is gone. An empty wave steals into my thought and I grow dizzy with my emptiness, grow hollow with the memory of my mother's mothering grace and her giving. I long for mother. Grandmother says sh sh sh you only have a fever you will soon be well. She wipes the sweat from my forehead and gives me something warm to drink.

A heaviness grows on my forehead pulling me away into a darkness so complete and I cry, my crying seems to come from my ears. The darkness is taking me away. A brilliant light falls into my eyes like breaking glass, so I close my eyes again and creep back into the darkness where perhaps my mother will come and find me.

Grandmother lifts me close to her. She sings about the river and its children. She says the river is wide like the sky and the sunset. In it all things begin and end. The river is horizon and cloud.

I scramble down the lemon tree knowing my mother is gone, swallowing my cry. I shout for mother, like blood in my mouth. There is only silence, then a whisper so faint from my mother, so distant. From far away Grandmother comes again dressed in water, saying this river is life. If you listen closely to the river you will hear a lullaby in its meandering banks, you will see birth. She whispers to me again with a firm voice saying do not count the stars in the sky, their beauty is not to be possessed in one's hand.

I look for my mother at the bottom of silent lakes. I watch a shadow creep slowly onto her face. I have wounded her with my forgetting, wounded myself. I long for the moment of birth.

Can you spell duck?

d u c k

The last letter sounds like someone scraping at the roof of my mouth . . . kkkkk

I spell the word again, and wait for another word from her. Again, d u c k, but she does not give me another word to spell. To regain her attention I raise my voice very loud, d u c k. She laughs and says, That is good, Zhizha.

Come and comb my hair, Zhizha, she says. With her left hand she extends an iron comb in my direction and a towel to put over her shoulders.

Are you sleeping, Zhizha? she calls in my direction, to wake me from dream. I sleep.

Zhizha.

I sleep.

There is a time of the year when everyone seems to remember me and whispers . . . Zhizha . . . Zhizha . . . very softly, banishing all those absences of my mother with this calling, then I seem to belong to everyone's mouth for a whole season. I am harvest. I am rain. I am river and rock. I am sky and earth. I am Zhizha.

At this time, the air is a sweetness of newly ripened things and I grow so joyous that my spirit soars and spirals, settling into one ray of golden light. My toes tingle in that warm earth as I help Grandmother spread water-filled seeds that are soft and slippery to dry under the sun. These are the seeds that are life, that hold secrets larger than themselves. At the moment of their birth their mothers trusted them with a secret, and they are tender with promise.

Zhizha, the people whisper, and I turn to hear. They are talking about the harvest.

Zhizha, my mother says, come and comb my hair.

I long to tell her that this endearment is no gift, that I desire no portions and fragments of her living. I long for her never to depart. I wish my mother would stay, but I meet her in dream. My heart beats angrily, and I think, besides, she named me after a stranger. A woman turned and gave my mother a greeting. She took her name.

Zhizha, she repeats, and I receive the comb.

I part her hair in the middle from her forehead to the back of her neck, creating a path. I send the comb through her hair. I move slowly in my parting, resting the comb down in her thicket of hair. I move to her left side and comb her hair straight down, comb it seven times. I am practicing my counting. After seven I start again and stop at six. Seven plus six equals thirteen. I keep the thirteen and start again. I comb five times. I add that to the thirteen. I have combed her hair . . .

Zhizha. I start suddenly.

Eighteen, I say.

What is that?

Thirteen plus . . .

Zhizha, comb the other side of my head, she says.

She takes the comb from my fingers and digs it abruptly into the hair on her right side.

Tiny black hairs fall against the towel as I comb, parts of her falling off. There are parts of her trapped in the comb. I pull these soft dying parts out and place them in the pocket of my dress, to secure a memory. I have trouble remembering my mother, so I work extra hard at it, alert to pick the parts of her which fall in my direction. Between my fingers I feel her hair, this hair which is part of me and of Grandmother. I touch the roots of her hair and at the bottom the hair is a shiny dark.

Grandmother's hair has turned white. Sometimes she says, Comb my hair, but often I am the one who says, Grandmother, may I comb your hair? I begin by parting the hair into two halves just like this and the roots are gray like smoke. Grandmother says her hair used to be black but the world has entered her too much and her hair has turned white.

I remember Grandmother and the feeling is like sunlight on my arms. The smoky grayness covering her head tells me too many things and I refuse to listen, instead I call out loud to her saying, Your hair is dark, Grandmother. It is not gray at all. I pull out one black hair from her head and place it in the middle of her palm, saying look. She looks at the hair and says, You are right, this hair is black like yesterday. Then she goes to the mirror and spoils all my dreaming. I follow her to the mirror and stand close to her.

Zhizha, my mother calls, stop pulling at my hair.

With that she removes the towel from her shoulders and looks at the many pieces of broken hair, very closely, then slowly proclaims . . .

You have broken my hair, Zhizha.

Mother, she calls. Mother.

But Grandmother is not home. Mother waits in her thin red dress, her arms resting on the windowsill, her hair parted, her eyes clear with tears. I wonder when next she will visit those long-ago places which sometimes pervade her face. When she turns, leaning her back against the lower part of the wall and her head against the window, she says, alluringly . . . Zhizha.

∾

Then there was the cease-fire and the women poured milk to the ground and welcomed the men home even when they had not seen them walk back, they sought them, their names and sheltering presences, their pounding hearts, and their many scars. The women had a new gaiety in their speech and their motions because something they thought had vanished had returned, somehow, with a scent they recognized as all their own. Not whole, this return. The surrender of weapons allowed the women to linger in their dreams, toward wakefulness, and touch their own lips in wonder. Waists thinned with anticipation, arms widened with joyful longing. They feared absence.

The wounded too arrived, lonely men lost and naked and thick with despair, unable to touch the edges of dream. These haunted many who had been wounded and could not nurture hope. Something about this day had taught them not despair, but shame. They hid their bodies beneath their bowed heads and folded shoulders. But the women sought them from their hiding because these men too they loved and let them in. They waited with their windows held open and their eyes embracing the sky, searching for those who were returning to plant new dreams on the ground, offering respite. The cease-fire meant that fear would be turned into celebration. They touched something in this new boundary, a new taste to joy, a new sound to dream. They rejoiced at the joys that tantalized them. Something. A newness, something hatched, pure and bright with surprise. Something not yet known, to be, almost, felt. A touch. The cease-fire had brought them a burst of hope. A whisper, a form, something held in the hand. Perhaps a necessity to living, a longing almost fulfilled, nearly complete. Places that would be their own, truly. A feeling that was shared and felt. A return. Something. Sparks of flame. A glitter of sunshine and incantations in the rain, chants and ululations. The absence of war. A fortunate illumination. Accustomed to fear and loneliness the people wept at the potential of freedom.

And the rain came. And the cease-fire. And the men were caught in the pouring water, but they walked on and threw away their weapons like worthless utensils, in easy courage and abandon. They had no more dreams to protect but their own bodies now scarred and harmless and sweet with passionate ambition. When some of the women offered their voices as shelter they dared not resist. These women had survived waiting. The men tumbled out of the sun, and they had brought women who had fought beside them.

These women had new names that the past did not echo, they had long arms and long legs and long voices. They laughed louder than the men because they had shared secrets with them. The women were strong and looked only at the sky where they said it was free. They would begin in the sky, not the earth. They would begin from there, so they removed the yellow roofs and the red roofs and tore them to the ground, with their own arms. They wanted to see something else, not this canopy of painted sky. They wanted to begin without shelter. And as for desire they knew something about that too. This emptiness, these bare roofs. These same women had killed farm dogs, white men, and grasshoppers.

Before this bustle of freedom, this cease-fire, ten years before, Muroyiwa had met Runyararo. Their child Zhizha slept in the room which had been created by the curtain with fading blue stars. In this tight space their lives would change completely while the war was fought and anticipations conjured.

Runyararo would be among those returning home from another direction altogether during this cease-fire, released, able to see her daughter again. She would miss the laughters shared by the returning and not see the battleground where a new belonging was talked of and understood, the wonderful rhapsody.

∾

twenty-three

My eyelids fight against the encroaching darkness. I turn and turn in my sleep. Night fills with the sounds of insects growing into the darkness, shrill whispers pitched in cries. I hear a vibrating call, a screeching sharp and persistent, followed by a chaos of whispers which prolong the night. I turn in my sleep, a chorus of sleep.

I wait for daylight but something carries me away into the darkness, into sleep. I drift in a bed of uneasy suspicion, and in my dream I meet myself participating in a ritual of death, dancing across a field of burning stumps. A shadow crosses my face and wakes me, but because whatever has chosen this night for its purpose intends to triumph it exerts its power over my eyelids through my sleep and I return to dream. A trembling sleep. I sleep a restless sleep traveling through mountains and rivers, through dark ominous skies, through hidden burial grounds, through groves of tangled trees. Then I wake suddenly, because some sound has reminded me of a deep oncoming sorrow, but because it has already been a night of sleep and wakefulness I turn again, and sleep. A smothering sleep, like death. My brow is wet with dreams. I turn and turn, longing for daylight.

A muffled cry struggles in the dark of the night followed by a silence so final I sleep. The cry rises again pitched and intense, from within me, circling high over my head, turning into a thick shadow. Again, I succumb to a deceitful sleep. A piercing scream enters my dream, moves past me into the darkness, climbs high in the sky. A shattering trembling scream from deep inside me, of blood and water in my crying. The shadow enters into me, enters my crying, covers my eyes with a heavy hand. My brow is wet with tears, wet with fear. My heart beats hard on my chest, seeks my dream and my waiting, banishes sleep. I hear my cry plead in the distance, then grow into a meander that leads farther into the darkness. My cry is silence and death. Night descends firmly into my wakefulness. The sound follows me, struggles to enter, pulling hard at my limbs. I descend deep into the earth. I struggle in the darkness.

I will die from the pounding of my heart which does not allow me to bend or move my arm but turns me into stone, fills my mouth with dry leaves, covers me in decay. My voice is caught in the midst of its awakening, unable to escape. My voice stands upright, a solid thing somewhere between my breasts splitting me in half. My voice seeks the moment of my birth, the secret in my name, the promise in my belonging.

I cry in my sleep, this sleep of death. Tomorrow has departed never to return, death has entered my dreaming entered my growing turned it into mud, and now I cry in one small whimper, cry quietly into my memory saying, whispering, I am the opposite of life. I am the distortion of birth. I am silence.

I long for daylight, for a remembrance of dawn. I see the sky covered in a thick purple hue more ominous than clouds of rain, a sky that has combined all the beauty and the evil of the world. It is a sky that claims two worlds.

I wait, in a purple sky.

My mouth threatens with a final drowning. The water moves, penetrates the darkness, pushes forward. A murmuring, a jarring motion, then a crash. I sink deep, beaten and helpless. My thought grows and grows into darkness, into night. I find my thought and my thought runs like a full and dirty stream on the side of a mountain not to be stopped but I follow my thought, wherever it goes, and my thought climbs trees, searches the bottom of rivers.

A snail moves blind beneath the green leaf and spreads a wet path over dying veins.

Father falls on my legs parted, spread on the cold floor.

He whispers, sings about a handful of sand gathered on the banks of rivers.

I cry for mercy, but my cry is silence. Mother, I cry in my sleep. A throbbing hard and horrid passes between my legs, searing, tearing. A wound fresh with blood grows into my chest. A seed grows on my navel, grows into a tree with firm roots that gather all the water from my stomach, pulls hard till my eyes are still, empty, and uprooted.

I fall from a tree, covered in thorns.

Father . . .

. . . blood in my crying.

He enters into me breathing hard. A snail spreads on stone, climbing upward, blind, pushing forward, its shell curled hard over its body, hiding from day in a deathly silence. The snail moves slow and searching over the rock, spreading through rock.

My stomach is hard like stone. I hear the sound of water breaking on rock.

In the darkness, he pulls hard at the roots of the tree, pulls at my navel. I cry between fierce fingers cradling my face . . . mother. A slow silent cry, futile.

I open my eyes.

Father . . .
Father . . .
Silence dark and still, vivid, like night sky.
Pushing. Pressing hard. He thrusts forward.
Father . . .

Night.
A hand dark and heavy descends over my face, over my eyes, tightens round my neck. My legs are crushed. My stomach is hard like rock.

He enters. I cry into the night but my cry returns to me and spreads down into my stomach like water, water, at the bottom of leaves, water, water beneath rock, water, water between my legs, water.

A snail moves over broken bones gathered on rock. A trail of saliva, of dew. My cry creeps from beneath rock.

Night.
My fingers are broken and crushed, white with bone.
Father . . .
My cry is death not life, softens, like stone breaking in water, softens, like saliva, softens, like rain.

I hear breathing, violent, breathing, on rock. A rigid silence.
Father . . . between my legs.

Wet between my legs. Blood-wet wetness. Not flowing wet. Slippery.
Not so loud.
He put mucus here, and blood . . .
Quiet.
He put mucus between my legs . . .
Quiet.
Am I going to die?
Quiet.
He broke my stomach . . .

He put blood between my legs.

The pain climbs upward through my chest. A searing cramping beneath my feet. An emptiness moves right through me, past me. A frantic
cry, then silence. Rain falling into dream. I rise from my crying, trembling.
It is like this. He is breathing hard spreading a humid air around my
face. A ringing awakening and something enters through my ears, ominous, and it will not depart. It spreads its darkness through me, past me,
feigning friendship. The sound curls inside me like a leaf, and dries. He
enters a dark breathing through my nose, thick with blood. He enters
through my crying saying very softly sh sh sh. The earth sways underneath, ruptures, and I fall into the darkness. My hand seeks the darkness
and finds a forehead grooved and moist, grooved and moist. He enters
into me, through me.

A tearing screaming then he sings to me a lullaby about tiny fishes
moving between reeds, and I must only think of them because they are

lonely and afraid and so little and if I don't think of them they might never grow but only swirl always in the green deep of the water.

Zhizha

He calls, breathing into my sleep. A sound grows beneath my body, like breaking rock and bone.

Crush.

Darkness and blood. My eyelids pulse, throb, tear. A trembling swelling lower lip then darkness so complete; there is no sound, no footsteps, no thundering shout, no tomorrow. I am alone. A cough rises from my stomach, grows through me while a thin ray of light slices my eyelids. My forehead swirls. A flood of piercing light enters my eyes and I cry. I joy to hear the sound of my crying. I have woken up, survived. Maybe I will live.

. . . tell grandfather?

No.

. . . tell grandfather?

No. It is death when such things are told.

Grandmother . . .

It is night.

I feel my eyelids fall while my tongue grows thick and heavy, pressed between my teeth. My tongue is hard like stone. I dare not cry or breathe. A shadow grows toward me. Father grows out of the shadow. I wait beneath the shadow which pushes forward in a violent thrust, crushing my legs.

mucus and saliva . . .

enters . . .

—————

It is night.

Blinding pain grows across my forehead, grows in my stomach, through me. My bones are broken and crushed. A cold hand presses hard on my knee, moves impatiently over my body, searching and digging. Fingers mumbling, muttering, cursing the darkness in a voice a husky quiet. A sudden shove, brutal and repeated. My knee breaks, slides sideways, contracts. My elbows are bruised and broken. He lifts my face, swings my head sideways, my head pressed down, my face cupped in his wide palm. Fingers enter into my eyes, mercilessly. He pushes sideways, sideways. He pushes at my broken knee. I cannot breathe. My forehead grows with a painful throbbing, grows into his waiting hand, grows into a rounded shell which he breaks and breaks with a clenched fist. I close my eyes and a black cloud spreads before the moon, like smoke.

A tortoise moves slowly forward, carrying a broken shell. It pulls its head inside, and hides. It pulls its legs in and hides. Its shell is broken and crushed because it has swallowed its own head, swallowed its own legs. Its stomach is hard like the earth, hard with the things it has swallowed. The neck twists and turns and swells slowly to one side. It totters slowly forward, wobbles on hidden legs, digs the ground slowly, frantically, burrows in the gathering earth. It hides, survives, moves slowly forward.

It is night.

Fingers reach and fold, thick with blood. I lie still. Then I hear my teeth fall from my mouth.

Father . . .

———

Father carries me in his hands, holds my head down with his fingers. Naked, I kick helplessly about. I cannot escape. I scrape the ground with weakening legs, with a dreadful torment, a feeble hope.

I open my mouth to fight or cry but my face is numb, dead. It has been hammered with a rock.

Father . . .

A cry waits in my stomach.

My feet are heavy with water. Darkness, thrusting forward, darkness. I lie still and wait. My legs are heavy with the darkness, cold and dead. I shift desperately forward. My body moves, turns, twists backward. Something falls deep and down in the darkness. I crawl forward, move in water. I crawl forward. I creep, I sleep, slowly wake. I sleep. The darkness tightens around my forehead, presses me to the ground with a cruel hand, and I am swallowed by the ground which meets me in a stirring echo rising, a mingling of lament, a torment of grief.

It is morning. My voice grows from inside me, broken and dry, lies still, waits to be remembered, rises soft like smoke, creeps out of the room, calls for mother, wakes.

A word does not rot unless it is carried in the mouth for too long, under the tongue.

∾

twenty-four

1980 spelled the end of loneliness and unfulfilled desire long kept. There were those who had the mischance to hope, though hope was another name for losing; losing was not quick like death. It was slow and priceless, especially to those who had cried for the end of loneliness, who had turned loneliness into conviction. In many ways they were convicts of a belief which had told them that to be merely human was enough, and that waiting was reason enough to keep living. Few understood what maxims made living wholesome. Few bothered to understand. Few were not ensnared by dream. They were captives.

Where ceremonies were discovered and celebrated, in the city, it became commonplace to see women carrying mirrors into the middle of the streets and crashing them onto the tarred ground while a passing beaten car swerved and its driver cursed and blew the horn. Rituals are born of adversity. Breaking mirrors in public places became a necessary ritual of abandon. Where mirrors could not be found empty bottles were broken to bring good fortune. There was something unfathomable in this easy act, courageous even. The sound and sight of breaking glass brought sharp edges to existence.

Breaking glass. Some said this was a ritual the women had invented in order to keep their longing ripe and ready, for they missed their men, pressed their eyes together in sleep to lock out desire and lock in pain, their lips together too to muffle despair, bit into their tongues for a taste of tenderness long gone, cupped their hands to shelter a spilling futility, to gather a nameless comfort, somehow, and finally, even in sleep, especially in sleep, crossed their legs for good fortune. It was a time for rites of woe. They missed their men, the women. Missed them, missed them.

History had become dazed and circular. Usually a hand-sized mirror was broken with one swing of the arm, but once, a woman was seen dragging a mirror the size of herself into the middle of the street while a crowd of children followed. The story was carried from mouth to mouth till it returned to the mouth of the same woman who had performed the marvelous act. The story told how this woman lifted her arms and heaved the mirror into the air like one possessed and brought it down with a dazzling crash. History was a spectacle, and this woman had found a new dream to make her own waiting real, original to her suffering and her particular endurance of anguish. The path left strewn with dangerous glitter was fair warning to oncomers that caution made living an art. And when the broken mirrors had become forgotten there was only the hurt lingering underneath coaxing words, just hurt and living and waiting, lingering, not forgotten.

1980 was a time to shorten distances to desire. Even those who had been restless and unconvinced found it necessary to open their windows an inch wider, to raise their voices a tone just enough to be heard above the hopeful rhythm of those who had clung to the frayed edges of dream. These anxious few, who felt threatened by the progress of desires they knew little about, saw nothing of, found it necessary to search their pockets for an extra coin that would purchase opportunity, if nothing else; being poor was part of the loneliness that accompanied waiting. Their voices hewn, frail and listless, their longing almost forgotten— they had waited.

~

CPSIA information can be obtained at www.ICGtesting.com
Printed in the USA
LVOW08s0148030816

498821LV00001B/51/P